I0737865

SHE AWAKENS

A DEBUT NOVEL BY

CAITLIN DENMAN

Copyright © 2021 by Caitlin Denman

All rights reserved.

No part of this book may be reproduced in any form or by any electronic
or mechanical means, including information storage and retrieval systems,
without written permission from the author, except for the use of brief
quotations in a book review.

I dedicate this book to my parents. Without your love and support this book wouldn't be possible

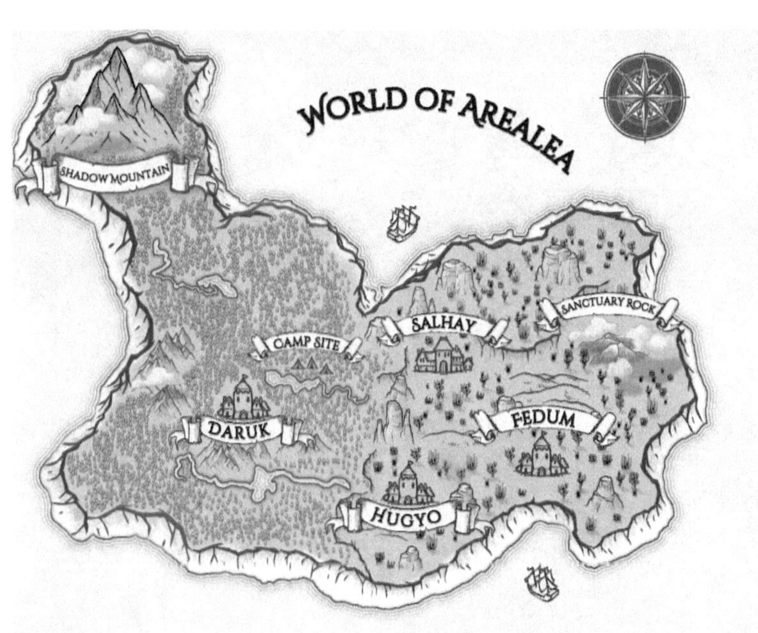

WORLD OF AREALEA
SHADOW MOUNTAIN
CAMP SITE
SALHAY
SANCTUARY ROCK
DARUK
FEDUM
HUGYO

PROLOGUE

Day of Destruction

GAZING OUT MY OFFICE WINDOW AT SHADOW MOUNTAIN, I still can't understand what has all my workers so spooked. It's only a mountain made out of rock and dirt, like all the other mountains we've blasted through to get us to this point.

I get they're superstitious, but this is getting ridiculous. What in all of Arealea could possibly cause these men to be so frightened of the boogieman?

I move from the window and begin pacing my small office. It's not much, merely a four-post canvas tent. There aren't even glass windows. Nothing but cut outs in the fabric opening to the world beyond and my men's pop up style camp. Like my office, my men live in canvas tents, which can be easily set up or dismantled as we travel and install new chunks of railroad.

Tonight, I left my bodyguard Silas to oversee the blasting

to the mountain's core. Usually such a thing wouldn't be necessary, but lately the men, even my own advisors, have been hysterical so I thought it best. The workers are full of stories of people living in the mountain and of curses and magic—like any of those are real. Then my advisors have the audacity to tell me I should listen to the workers and go around the mountain. Has everyone around me gone mad? But even with everything going on, I don't think any of my men would do something to sabotage this project. Over the years though, I've learned it's better to be safe than sorry.

What am I going to do? If this keeps up, it's on track to end up costing me more money and I'm already losing money I don't have.

Bam!

Bam!

Bam!

The charges are blasting off exactly as they should be. As I walk back to my window, I see the typical shaking of the ground and the puff of dust coming out the entrance we created weeks ago in the mountain face.

With the blasting over, I turn to walk to my desk. There are bills waiting to be paid, but something catches my eye as I pivot, forcing me to turn back. I see a human sized shadow coming out of the mountain entrance.

Then another.

And another.

Until a mass of people burst out of the mountain, then I hear it. Screaming.

Men are screaming and running like they're being chased from the bowels of hell itself.

More shadows pour out of the hole than should even be possible. There were only a handful of people authorized to be down there during the blasting, only the bare minimum.

Now from my vantage point 500 feet down the mountain, I can see there has to be a hundred people flooding out of the dark void. Most of those shadows are moving too fast, inhumanly fast.

As I watch I see man after man swallowed up by this swarm of shadows. One man falls to the ground as a dark wave of figures crashes over their prostrate bodies.

What's going on? What's happening to those men and who are all those extra people?

Finally, I move.

I rush over to my desk, pull open my top drawer, and grab my pistol.

As I race over to the tarpaulin entrance to my office, I check to make sure the pistol's loaded and walk back over to my canvas door, throwing open the fabric.

The last thing I would expect to see is what's in front of me.

A stunning woman blocks my path.

As my eyes drift down her curvy, tight body and I see her long brown hair ,which flows down the length of her back all the way down to her butt. Her face is interesting. Her chin and cheeks are angular but her eyes, while being blood red, are deep pools calling to me to follow her to the ends of Arealea. Below her chin, I see a rose necklace poking out atop her ample bosom.

I am completely captivated by this woman.

In the edges of my vision, I see the camp where my workers live is on fire and my men are being slaughtered by some kind of creatures. They can't be humans. These beasts, for lack of a better word, are moving too fast for me to see exactly what they are. Their frames are human-like, but their accelerated movements are too precise to be human, but none of it matters, compared to the woman standing in front of me.

When I refocus on the woman, she has her head cocked to the side. The stare reminds me of when I see an interesting bug I'm about to smash. My eyes drift down, and I notice a beautiful sword by her side, which I didn't see initially.

Engraved down the blade are strange dark, glittering black runes, like nothing I've ever seen before, and the hand guard is fashioned to give the impression thorns are wrapping around her hand.

Why would such a stunningly beautiful woman be holding something so deadly? What is she doing here? Did she run out of the mountain? Why am I only now thinking of this? I feel like I'm under some kind of trance.

My gaze shifts back to her face and I don't even think to raise my gun towards her before I feel that exquisite blade slice through me. I grab for my stomach, trying to staunch the bleeding, and focus on her eyes. I didn't notice before, but those eyes show a fire dancing in them, pushing to crawl out and consume us both.

I raise my gun.

I am about to die, but at least I can take her out with me.

I pull the trigger, the gun goes off with a loud bang, but as I fall to my knees from blood loss, I realize the woman is gone. She was right in front of me less than a second ago and now she's disappeared? *How did this happen? How did she move so fast? How did she dodge my shot?*

I collapse on the ground and then Silas appears right inside of my tent. I hold my arm out, trying to reach for him, stretching my hand toward help.

I'm dying. I know I am. There's only so much blood a human body can lose before death pulls you under. I've already lost too much. No one can help me, I know this, but I can't ignore my body's survival instinct, so I call out to Silas.

"Silas, please help me!"

"Wharton, hang on! I'm coming!" he shouts.

But before he can make it over to me, everything goes still, silent, and black

1

———

ATTINA

High in the treetops, I gaze out over our town. The weight of our task places a heavy burden upon my shoulders, especially today. James and I provide meat for our town, Daruk. No matter what, if we're getting along or we're fighting, we head out daily to hunt game.

Every day, we check traps, which we set the day before. We have ten traps in total, which we check religiously, scattered around the outskirts of town. Our snares are only big enough to catch small game such as rabbits, squirrels, and the like. But it's not always enough food to provide for the entire town.

In the cold hard winters, when critters are scarce, our food stores are what keep the town alive. The good thing is while James and I hunt for meat most of the rest of our townspeople raise anything small enough to not take up much room like pigs, goats, chickens, and geese. While we don't have to provide food for everyone, I still feel it is my responsibility to keep our food stores brimming with meat. You never know when some sickness will run through our town's animals.

Once we check our traps, we invariably end up in the same tree. It's the tallest one anywhere in or around town. Our routine is simple. After we check all of our snares, we tie up the small game we've gathered high in the tree, so no other predators can reach it easily, and then we climb to the tippy top and search for signs of bigger game.

Even as children, whenever we were out on one of our adventures, James would regularly tell me someday we would marry, and this day is no different. For about the fifteenth time, he quietly glances intensely at me as we ascend the tree. The silence between us is stifling. Usually, there isn't ever a lull in our conversations, but today things have been off, almost strained for some reason.

Most days, I would try to figure out what is going on with him, but today I don't have it in me. For the past week, I haven't been getting nearly enough sleep. The strangest things have been happening to me. I've been waking to find things floating around my room—my things. I open my eyes and small things like pens, my clock, a brush, and even clothes I left on the floor are floating above my head, circling my bed.

At first, I thought I was simply having a strange dream because I would wake up once throughout the night, see the objects floating, and immediately fall back asleep. Then each morning I would check around my room, but all my things would be exactly where I left them the night before.

This morning was different though.

I didn't wake up in the middle of the night last night. I slept peacefully throughout the night this time, but when I opened my eyes this morning, all the objects I'd thought I'd dreamt of were soaring around my room over my bed again.

I screamed and somehow fell out of bed, and as soon as my butt hit the ground all the things which were floating seconds ago fall from the air, scattering all over my room. Not two seconds later, my father was pounding on my door asking what happened. I made up an excuse at the time to appease him and keep him from asking too many questions, but now I'm left with a slew of questions myself.

What's happening to me?

Can I stop whatever this is?

How do I hide what is happening? No one can know about this. If the townspeople find out I have some sort of magical powers everyone would panic. The only people in Arealea who have powers are the Fae. Even though the townspeople have known me my entire life, their hatred of the Fae and magic is bottomless. I know I would become a pariah if anyone found out about whatever these powers are. Just as I feel myself being dragged down the rabbit hole of anxiety, James finally breaks the silence, "I can't wait until I can make you my wife." It isn't the words that are so shocking, it's the way he feasts his eyes on me and the conviction in his words. I've never heard this kind of cocksureness in his voice before, not once in the twelve years we've known each other.

His declaration shocks me to such an extent, as I reach up to the next branch, I stumble and miss it completely. My body jerks a little as I stabilize myself, but there's no harm done. James's intake of breath is the only way I know he saw me slip. James has ceaselessly tried to protect me, oftentimes too much. I can take care of myself. I don't need to be coddled or protected. This tendency of his has caused many fights over the years.

When I finally climb to the top of the tree, James is already waiting for me. His eyes are wide, his brows are raised, and a simpering smile is smeared on his expectant face... I shake my head. "Why do you always say you want to marry me?"

At my question, his mouth drops open. "You have no idea, do you?" I purse my lips. "Attina, you are my best friend. We've been friends for as long as I can remember. Our families already love each other, and being with you would be as easy as breathing; and just so you know, I plan to be breathing for the rest of my life."

I stare into the distance atop this monstrous tree trying to muster up some courage for what I need to say. My stomach drops knowing this moment could change our lives forever. How do I tell him I'm not ready for this kind of commitment? Will he hate me if I turn him down? Do I even want to turn him down? I mean, I know I love him, but am I *in* love with him? I'm not sure. The instant these thoughts run through my mind, something extraordinary happens.

A big, clamoring noise, like tree branches slamming against each other, draws our attention away from the conversation. To the east, a whole flock of ravens swarm up and out of the trees. Ravens are big birds, which aren't easily spooked, so what in the world could've frightened them so thoroughly? I peek at James and simply by the expression on his face, the way his eyebrows are drawn together and by his thinned lips, I know he's as confused as I am.

"We have to check it out. Hopefully, it's a deer, we haven't seen one in about a month, the town could use it", I say without taking my eyes off the tree line.

He turns to me. "There's no way that's a deer. When have you ever seen a deer cause that kind of ruckus?" A wicked grin appears on his face. He wiggles his eyebrows and says, "Unless it's mating season."

I take a deep exasperated breath and release it, annoyed because he's not taking the situation seriously. "You know very well the mating season for deer isn't until the fall, so don't be ridiculous. And if you don't think it could be a deer, then that's all the more reason to check it out. Whatever caused that kind of reaction is too close to town already."

He rolls his eyes. "Yeah, yeah. Let's go, but whatever you do, stay behind me." He drops out of the tree, and at first glance it appears like he's fallen, but then I realize somehow in the last second, he grabbed onto a low hanging branch and propelled himself toward the ground, never losing a step. He's focused and elegant, and I've never been able to be so graceful myself. I'm a klutz, always have been, always will be.

By the time I make my way down the tree, James is already so far ahead of me I to run to keep within sight of him. As soon as my feet touch dirt, I race past our catch of the day tied up in the tree and keep running, crashing through the forest to gain ground on him. I know it's the opposite of what James told me to do, but honestly how else am I supposed to keep up with mister long legs McGee?

After a couple of minutes, he stops, turns around, and waits for me to overtake him. I slowly creep up, nervously grasping onto the necklace my mother left me when she died. It's nothing fancy, just a chain with a charm of a red rose in bloom. The nervous habit of mine rearing its ugly head as I fidget with it, fondling it between my fingers. I worry at the necklace more than I like to admit. Even the paint on the edges of the rose has rubbed off a little over the years.

"I thought I said to be quiet," he hisses.

I shrug my shoulders. "It's your fault you left me behind." James rolls his eyes, turns around, and continues his trek at a slow, stalking walk. Now, since I've caught up with him, I'm able to keep right behind him as we move. I put one foot in front of the other, making sure to only step where he steps. After a few minutes, I can tell we're close to where the commotion was.

Not paying any attention to what's going on around me, I run smack dab into his hard muscled back. I take a step back as I rub my forehead and notice the forest has gotten too quiet. My gaze moves all around the forest, scanning for any signs of life. I'm seeking for signs of a bird gliding through the sky, a squirrel crawling up a tree, but I see nothing. I've never seen the forest this devoid of life before. I'm shocked. I whisper James's name and tug on his elbow.

He ignores me and keeps walking. I follow until he turns his head and mouths "stay here" and I do exactly as he says. He slowly stalks around a thick gnarly pine tree to our left. As soon as James is out of sight, I hear "Shit!" escape his mouth.

Without thinking, I take off running after him. I pass the pine tree and slam right into his backside, again. Shaking my head, I peer around him. I begin to ask him what happened, but my mouth closes instantly. I have no idea where to start. What I see before me is too unnerving. The scene in front of me is one, which will stay with me for the rest of my life.

Ahead of us is a man, if you can call him such a thing, clawing his way towards us on the ground. His fingers are coated in black dirt, and they're digging into the soft earth. He must've been at this for a while because it appears a few of his fingernails are missing from the effort of pulling his body along. His legs are badly broken and parts of his thighs are missing. I assume it's because he's dragged them so long, based on the blood trail he left in his wake. Without putting much thought into it, I push James aside and take a step to help the man, but James grabs me tightly by the waist and pulls me back against his hard, muscular body.

"Wait, just watch."

Shocked, I fight against my instinct to help and listen to James instead. My breath catches when the man's eyes lock onto mine.

Gazing down at his face I can tell he must have been a handsome man at one point. He still has stunning blue eyes and what would be a strong jaw line, but it's now broken. One side of it hangs away from his face and his nose is missing completely. As I take in his features fully, a gasp escapes me and a shiver wracks my body.

The man cries out the most guttural, nasty cry I've ever heard break free from a human. The man, if you can even call him such a thing, since he doesn't appear to be human anymore, doubles his effort to crawl over to us. I stumble backwards, expecting James to be there, but I fall on my butt instead. The thing snatches onto my ankle and our eyes lock as he tries to pull my leg toward his gaping maw.

Then, out of nowhere a machete is thrust down through the top of the man's head, piercing all the way through to the ground. It slumps forward and stops moving. I break my eyes away from the man's lifeless head and glance up to see James's triumphant face looming over me.

"What the hell was that?" I shout.

James ignores me, pulling his machete out of the man's head and before I realize what he's doing, he brings his machete down in one big swing and chops the head clean off. Leaning down, he grabs the head up by its sandy matted hair.

James glances down at me. "I'm not sure, but we need to get this back to the town elders. They'll know what to do." He turns around and walks off, leaving me to my thoughts.

What was that man?

His legs were almost falling off, how was he able to pull himself around like that?

Wouldn't an injury like that have killed him?

And even with such a mangled jaw, he tried to bite me. Why would he try to bite me?

Quickly, I pry my ankle out of the now dead and decapitated man's grasp, and I hop up off of the ground and chase after him as he heads back to our tree.

We finally make it back to our huge tree and before James can do it—he's holding the man's head and I don't even want to look at it—I move to untie the catch and hear a wet thump behind me. Before I know what's happening, James has me turned around and pushed up hard against the trunk of our tree, the man's head now gone from his hands.

"What are you doing?" I ask breathlessly, feeling heat rise to my cheeks.

He stares deeply into my eyes and I see his eyes are determined. "We will figure this out, Attina. We're going to be okay. I want a family and to live happily ever after. You are my family and my happily ever after."

Without warning, James's lips crash hard on mine, shocking me. His mouth claims mine. He sucks and pulls at my lips, and the sensation puts me into a deep trance. I close my eyes as our lips explore each other's. Then, all of a sudden he moves away.

I'm left reeling as he finishes untying our catch, leaving me against the tree breathing heavily. That was more than just a stolen kiss. I shake myself out of my stupor and grab the bag with our day's catch from James' hand.

"Come on, let's hurry home," I mutter as I leave him behind to grab the head. I focus on putting one foot in front of the other. How could he grab me that way? Like I belong to him? He knows I want to go on adventures but he's planning to settle down with me? I'm not sure how I feel about all of this.

Walking back to town, there is a tangible tension between us, which wasn't there before the kiss. It's not until we make it back to town does the tension between us lifts. The only reason the air clears between us though, is because at the town entrance we're intercepted by Nathan, clad in his usual brown, hole ridden robes.

Nathan is one of our town elders and a family friend of mine. Some days, Nathan meets us at the town entrance after hunting, purely to say hi and see how the hunt went, and today seems to be one of those days.

He peers down at the head in James's hand and quickly grabs him by the elbow and rushes him off into the town hall. Neither of them give me a second glance and leave before I have time to say a word to either of them. So with their dismissal, I take our catch to the town marketplace and make my way home.

By the time I make it home, Father is gone. More than likely he was already inside the town hall when Nathan whisked James in there, so I am left to my own thoughts for the rest of the night. After a few hours by myself, I start to calm down after the events of today and am finally able to think of everything that has happened more rationally. To my surprise, the man we found in the forest today is not on the forefront of my mind.

I can't get our kiss out of my head. Maybe James just got caught up in the moment when he kissed me? That must be it. He said a bunch of mushy nonsense, became engrossed in what was going on, and got carried away. Raising my hand, I touch my lips and I realize I hope he doesn't remember everything that happened between us this morning. But in all reality, why in Arealea wouldn't he remember something like that? But a girl can hope. I absolutely do not want things to be different. I like how things are between us and don't want it to ever change. As the thought leaves my head, I feel my body relax, and think to myself *I'm never going to get a good night's rest after everything that happened today.* I close my eyes and drift to sleep.

2

ATTINA

As my hand reaches to the next branch, the rough bark digs into my skin, and the pain grounds me. My boot grabs deep into the spiraling texture of the tree and the coffee-colored husk scrapes down my body against my usual bland clothing. Today, I wore my typical hunting clothes, soft gray wool pants, a T-shirt, and light coat to match. They might not be pretty, but they're comfy and practical. I sit on one of the top tree branches glancing up and out at the beautiful landscape before me.

From this high up, I can see all the way back to Daruk. The town itself is built right into a mass of pine trees. The original builders cleared away barely enough trees to build the few structures we needed. As the town slowly grew, only enough trees were felled as were absolutely necessary. All of the town's structures were constructed lower than the surrounding trees and the pine needles of the trees were used to thatch all the roofs, which helped make our town semi camouflaged.

From afar, the town could be mistaken for a low spot in the forest. A small road only big enough for a horse and cart runs right through the middle of town. Right inside the town entrance on one side is the town hall, on the other is our marketplace. At the marketplace, townspeople can sell the wares they grow or make. Small, scattered houses finish out the town. It's not much, but it's all I've ever known. It's my home.

Growing up in such a small town meant I grew up in a tight knit community. Only about fifty people reside there, but it's slowly been growing year after year. When I was a child, there were less than half a dozen kids. Now, twice the number can be seen running around, playing throughout town. My hometown is the only inhabited town in a hard two-day ride, which means everyone I ever knew or wanted to know lived here.

The town is surrounded by a dense, green forest. Grass and leaves coat the forest floor creating a soft bed, and the tree canopy intertwines so tightly in spots it blocks out the sunlight. This makes it a perfect spot for afternoon naps and childhood games. The forest became my playground growing up.

Living in a tight knit community was great, but a town like mine—where everyone knew each other and where everyone was in someone else's business—was suffocating. So suffocating, that growing up I was rarely found in town. Most of my formative days were spent in the forest playing imaginary games, having magical adventures in far off places, or playing hide and seek with James. I've always loved my hometown, but I'll forever yearn for something more.

Growing up, I only had one real friend, James. Even though he was seven years older than me, we did everything together. We'd go on adventures and play in the woods like there wasn't a care in the world.

Exploring with him was some of the best times I can remember as a child. The first time we met was fourteen years ago, and it will be etched into my mind forever. I was about six-years-old, which would've made James thirteen at the time.

A few months prior, he'd stumbled into our town half dead. The town took him in at once, but there was one problem—he wouldn't talk. From the moment he showed up, not one word was uttered from his lips. The adults put his silence off as him being scared or shy. He was immediately adopted by a couple in town, who couldn't have children of their own.

After a few weeks of fattening James up and making him feel safe, he still wouldn't talk. His adoptive parents thought it would be best for him to socialize with the few children in town, and maybe it would bring him out of his shell.

Once a week, a new child would visit James at his adoptive parent's house. Child after child visited, but he showed no sign of change. They started out by introducing him to children his own age, but as the weeks passed, there was a smaller and smaller pool of children he hadn't met. Everyone began giving up on him and started assuming the shock of what happened to him was utterly too much and he would stay a mute for life. Then came my turn.

I remember being terrified to meet him. There hadn't been a new person in town in my entire life. What if he hated me? What if he was mean? What if he picked on me? None of the other kids really interacted with me, so would this one be different?

I was the daughter of a town elder, so the other kids kept well away from me like I had a plague. I guess they thought I would tattle on them. I remember the knot of worry in my stomach as my father and I walked into James' house.

When we walked in, he was sitting at the family table coloring. He was so fixated on coloring he didn't even notice when we entered the room. Father bent down behind me and pushed me forward,

"Go say hi, Pumpkin."

I was nervous, but I walked over to the table and sat down next to James anyway. I wasn't sure if he knew I was there or not, but it wasn't until I said, "Hello, I'm Attina," that I got any sort of reaction. When he heard my voice, a glint flashed behind his eyes like something clicked inside his head. He immediately stopped coloring and lifted his eyes toward me.

The look in his eyes was gloomy; detached and so dark it both haunted and scared me. But when our gazes locked and I smiled at him, my fear left me completely. I saw something in his stare change and his face brightened as he focused on me.

His eyes widened and his mouth dropped open in what I can only describe as a surprised expression. As he took me in his shoulders dropped and I could almost see his body physically relax. Then, his gaze traveled around the rest of the room, taking in his parents and my father. He didn't seem like he was surprised to see them in the room, but the sparkle in his eyes made me think this was the first time he was truly seeing them, or rather connecting with their presence.

He peered back to me, handed me a crayon, and from then on we were inseparable. It was so easy back then. One crayon shared and we became friends, just like that, much easier than the way things are now. It took a couple of days of my father and me visiting, but he eventually opened up and started talking.

The one drawback, however, was once I got him to start

talking, he wouldn't stop. Over the next few months James's adoptive parents found out he was from a native people, who had lived in the forest at the base of Shadow Mountain for centuries, living harmoniously with the Fae. The tribe kept to itself and cultivated their plot of land growing vegetables and grain, only hunting enough for everyone in the tribe to eat. The Fae let them live in peace for centuries. Then one day, the Fae stormed their tribe and gave their chief an ultimatum, subservience or death.

Subservience meant handing over their children so the Fae could train them to become lifelong servants to the Fae. The chief of James's tribe refused this "offer", which insulted and angered the Fae, and it ended in all out war. I say war, but in actuality it wasn't a war, it was a massacre.

The native's weapons were no match against the Fae's strength, speed, and magic. Within minutes, the entire tribe was all but obliterated. James's mother managed to run away with him before the Fae found them, but his mother was not one to run and hide. She was a tough, loving, tribal woman and would never let her loved ones suffer alone, so she fought to the death for her family.

After finding a safe hiding spot for her son she told him to stay hidden until she came back— but she never returned.

James found his way back to his tribe only to find everyone slaughtered, including his mother. Then he'd wandered for days searching for any sign of human life, struggling to survive, praying to the Gods to find help. Finally, by some miracle, he had stumbled half dead into our town, and salvation.

James was the first person in town to interact with the Fae and live to tell the tale. An exuberant amount of questions were brought to him, even at such a young age. Were they monsters? Did they know about the outside world? Should we fear them? James couldn't answer many of our elders' questions, but he was able to give a broad description of them.

The Fae who came to his tribe were extremely human-like, except for their eyes and ears. Their eyes were bright colors not seen in humans––reds, yellows, and even purples. Their ears were strange and exaggeratedly pointed. Other than those distinguishing features, we wouldn't be able to tell them apart from humans, unless they fought or used their magic.

They fought with intensified strength and speed. Some of the Fae used their magical powers in the melee. Some could control fire or water, some even had the power to bore right into a man's mind and make them their puppet. Being so young James told our elders he remembered the Fae being angry and out for blood.

Throughout the years, James and I became best friends. I'm not sure what it was about me he took a liking to, but after our first meeting we became inseparable, and our big age difference led him to become a friend and a mentor.

James remembered what he'd learned from living in a tribe. He taught me everything he knew, how to tell if plants were poisonous, and how to lay traps for small game. He was the first one to show me how to climb a tree and who was there when I fell out of a tree and cut my shin wide open.

Ever the teacher, even when I fell out of that tree, he calmed my hysterical cries and showed me how his people sutured up deep wounds like mine. I would forever have a nasty scar to remind myself of the day, but I was able to walk home by myself without much pain.

Once I'd mastered all those skills, he taught me how to

shoot a bow, and it quickly became my passion. From the first moment James put a bow in my hands I felt something special, a connection to it, like the bow was an extension of my arms. Shooting an arrow became empowering to me. I soon moved on from shooting targets to shooting small game.

I was a natural with the bow and moved up to bigger game, and eventually to birds. Shooting birds was the hardest because I learned I had to shoot them out of the air while they were on the move. The trick was you had to know where the bird would be before it got there, which took practice and experience. Learning how to shoot finally gave me a purpose. Between James teaching me his skills, and Father teaching me everything he knew over the years, I came to feel like a force to be reckoned with.

Hunting with James became a daily ritual for me. Every single day I could count on him to be by my side rain or shine, but after we came across the Solis the other day, everything changed. The past few days I've had to hunt for our town all on my own while James worked on something with the town elders.

I have always been perfectly capable of hunting on my own. In the back of my mind I had begun to realize, I was beginning to miss him. He keeps creeping through my mind during the day. I miss his smile and his presence more than I care to acknowledge. When did these feelings begin? I've perpetually brushed off each and every attempt he made to woo me over the years, but now I don't know how I feel.

The following day I wake to the same objects floating around my room but today it doesn't scare me like it did the past couple days. I'm not sure why, but it doesn't. I climb out of bed, and like the previous days, as soon as I'm fully awake, everything floating drops to the ground. Just like the previous mornings, I pick them up and set them back in their places before getting ready for the day.

Today our entire town is to gather in the small hall. The elders want to tell everyone what happened to James and me in the forest and discuss what to do about it. My father is also one of the town elders. He became an elder because he is one of the most trusted people in town and one of the original founders. Growing up, Father told me he built our house for Mother and me and the town soon developed around us.

Over the years, he'd helped almost everyone somehow or another; whether it was helping to build their own house or helping to provide some much needed food to new residents, he'd consistently been there. So, when the town was big enough to need elders, he'd been an obvious choice. Unsurprisingly, my father had already left our house when I set out on my walk to the hall. But as soon as I walk out of our front door I hear my name shouted.

"Attina!"

I know this particular voice almost as well as I know my own. When I turn around, James is running down the road toward my small cottage. For as long as I can remember, he's had an interest in becoming a town elder.

He's constantly shown his worth by providing meat throughout the years and volunteering to help anyone in town. James has even been helping the town elders with this upcoming meeting and I'm sure he's learning what he can about the man we came across in the woods. With him being groomed to be a town elder, it means he's been extremely busy getting things ready for this meeting, so the last time I saw him was a few days ago on our last hunt.

This time, while I watch him run up to my cottage, I take a good look at him for the first time in what feels like a long time. Only yesterday, I thought of how James and I met, and now, while scrutinizing him like this, I can finally see the difference from the boy back then to the man walking towards me now.

He's seven years older than me, and he's already turning into a man. Today, like every day, he's wearing his hunting clothes. A shirt and pants he fashioned out of leather from goats over the years. He says they help his body move freely, and today I can definitely tell those leathers fit his body well. His muscles have started to become more toned and defined. He no longer has a little boy's build to his body. Now he's filled out in all the right places. His jaw is more defined, his long, dark hair, which reaches past his shoulders, is tied back in a ponytail. His big ears are poking out the sides of his head, but it's his eyes that truly catch my attention. Those eyes of his stun me. I've always loved the color of them but now they're piercing. Even though they are brown, they carry a variety of different hues. They seem almost iridescent. I shake myself back to the present and give him a whistle.

"Hey big ears. What are you doing here?"

When James finally reaches my front door, he ignores my insult and takes me by the elbow. "I came to escort you to the town meeting, little lady."

I roll my eyes. "I'm not little and I don't need a babysitter."

"I know, but your father asked me to pick you up from home." A huge smirk spreads across his face like he's won some prize.

As we walk by the building, which holds the town's food stores, my annoyance at the situation pours out. "I don't know why he continues to think I need a babysitter," I mumble under my breath.

James peers sideways at me and then pushes me into the alley next to the building, taking me completely by surprise. "What are you doing? Why—"

When I gaze up at him, I see an intensity I don't often see in his eyes, he pushes me up against the building's outside wall, putting both of his arms on either side of my head making sure I can't leave. His face is mere inches from mine. His eyes move to my lips and his breathing increases.

"Attina, Silas loves you. With everything going on, he wants to make sure you are safe, and he trusts me. You're more precious to people than you realize."

He puts one hand on my cheek caressing my face till he reaches my chin and gently grasps it lifting my face towards his. I take my chance and scoot out of his grasp, I'm able to take a few steps and turn around, when I peer back, his forehead is resting against the wall.

He lets out a big sigh and turns to me. "You know we will be married one day, you could at least act like you want more than just a playmate."

I place my hands on my hips and tap my foot. "You are the one that knows we will be married one day, not me. I am the writer of my own story, not you." Then I turn around and run the rest of the way to the town hall, but no matter how fast I run I can't get the hurt expression on James's face out of my head.

3
___

ATTINA

WHEN I ARRIVE AT THE DILAPIDATED BUILDING WE CALL OUR town hall, I have to bend over and catch my breath. My breathing is erratic, and I already feel like there are knives lodged in my lungs and a split in my side. I make a mental note, I truly need to get in better shape.

When I finally collect myself, I peek up to the hall. It's not much of a building, only four walls making up one big room. It doesn't even have doors on it. Some years ago, we had re-purposed the doors to help a couple in the community. They needed the doors more than a town hall building needed them.

The hall is already full of people and everyone is milling about, talking to each other. As I walk to the front of the room where I know my father will be, I can hear a couple words from these conversations... Solis... where... I thought it was over... I reach for my necklace and hold it as I walk. It's weird hearing someone talk about the Solis.

The Solis are monsters in a story told to us as kids to scare us into being well behaved. They weren't real, or so I thought. I can't understand it. People are having a serious conversation about the Solis? What's happening here? Before I can contemplate it too much, I see my father at the front of the hall.

He's a big, daunting man. He has a broad muscled chest, and when he walks into a room, everyone takes notice. Growing up together I remember he always had short, thick jet-black hair, but as he's matured, gray hairs have peppered throughout. The rest of his features are somehow soft, while being rough at the same time. He seems like a big scary bear, but in reality he's as gentle as a teddy bear.

I call out to him waving my hand in the air. "Dad!" I yell, and immediately release my necklace to run over to him. Like every day, my father takes pride in his appearance. He always manages to have the nicest tunics and today is no exception. He's wearing a dark purple tunic which he fashioned himself specifically to match his muscled physique and broad shoulders.

"Hey pumpkin," he says warmly.

I scrunch my nose and his laugh brings a twinkle to his bright aquamarine eyes, the same eyes I have, and the only physical trait I acquired from him. The years have been tough on Father.

It's been only the two of us my whole life; my mom died a few days after giving birth to me. Growing up, he had to be my father and mother, which was a full time job. Yet, he still made time to help run our town.

Today though, the years seem to be weighing on him more than usual. The lines in the corner of his eyes seem deeper and although his tunic was fashioned to fit him perfectly, now his clothes seem to hang off him looser. I only saw him this morning at breakfast and there is already an immense change in him. My stomach drops. Whatever this is about must be bad.

I walk into his open arms and hug him with everything I have. "Dad, what's going on? Why the huge meeting? Whatever's happening can't be so bad the whole town would be affected, could it?" My father's face takes on the grave expression he regularly wears when trouble is coming. His brows furrow and his lips purse like he's just sucked on a lemon. He should never play poker; his every thought shows on his face.

"Well Attina, I guess we'll find out. I saved you a seat next to James in the front row. Go ahead and have a seat, we're about to get started."

When I turn to walk to my seat, I see James is already sitting in his next to mine. His eyes are wide, and a slight smirk is on his lips, giving his face an expectant air. I'm still furious with him, but he is my best friend and I know I can't stay mad at him for long. Before I can sit down, he stumbles out, "Attina... I'm... I don't know—"

I hold out my hand to stop him mid-sentence. "Relax. You need to stop trying to own me, and everything will be fine between us." I give him the best smile I can muster.

"I wish you'd realize how great you are."

I cross my arms and glare down at him. "Which is for me to find out, not for you to push on me. You're my best friend and that's all I want."

"Okay. But I'm still gonna wait for you."

"Don't!" I snap.

His lips curve up and a thin, wicked grin spreads across his face, but only for an instant. Then his face relaxes and he replaces the wicked grin with a wink and a soft, sweet smile. The crack of the gavel rings out three times throughout the hall, a sign for everyone to take their seats. I take my seat next to him and hold my breath as the man up on the little stage at a podium clears his throat.

I know the man well. Nathan has spent many nights at my house through the years going over town business with my father. Today he's abandoned his normal hole filled robes and is wearing a stately plain black robe that drapes all the way to the ground. I knew this meeting was important but if Nathan is this dressed up it must be more important than I originally thought. I run my eyes over his body scanning for any other differences in his appearance, but he still seems like the same Nathan I grew up with. He has a head full of gray hair, but has some of the kindest green eyes I've ever seen. He also gives me candy every time I see him and no matter how old I've gotten, I've always loved it. Nathan has invariably been such a strong person. Someone the town could continuously rely on to lead. Now, his usual smiling face is gaunt and gray. Being in the front row, I can almost see his body shudder under the stress, which immediately gets my attention.

Then he starts talking and his usually deep confident voice is shaky. "Well, I'm sure you're all wondering why we called this town meeting." There's a murmur from the room. Nathan pushes on. "James and Attina were able to shed light on what's been happening outside of town. It seems as if the Solis have progressively gotten worse. The big cities must be uninhabitable by now." There is an audible intake of breath in the room before everything becomes silent.

I quickly swing back and forth, scanning around the room, confused as to what's happening. The Solis are real? What's going on? How is such a thing possible? My quick movements draw Nathan's attention. "I know this must be a huge shock to those of you who were born here or were extremely young when we settled into this town. Everyone who moved to this community agreed long ago we wouldn't talk about the Solis unless it was deemed necessary. For those of you who don't know, the Solis were once humans like you and me, until the Fae showed themselves. I know some stories of the Solis have leaked out over the years and well, they're all true." Women start screaming and children start crying. At this point, Nathan lowers his head and raises his hand. "Please, I know some of you are having a hard time with this right now but please hear me out."

He clears his throat and starts again. "To your next question, yes, magic exists and it's extraordinarily awful. All the Fae want is to rule Arealea by conquering every last human. They will kill us, turn us all into slaves, or wait for us to be changed by the Solis."

"The Solis have one thing on their minds—death and destruction. No one knows for certain why they were created. If I had to venture a guess, I'd think they were created to wipe out the rest of the human race completely. We might not know why they were created, but we do know who created them."

"The Solis were created by the Fae King, Henrik."

"Henrik used blood magic to bring these unnatural things to fruition. The venom in their bite kills the soul, but reanimates the body. The venom is the real trick to this spell; it is laced with Henrik's own blood. After a human is bitten, Henrik's magic enters the body, kills the human, and then his spell resuscitates the body without the soul. From then on, the body's only reason for functioning is to find their food, humans. When the Solis have found their food, and taken a bite of it, the cycle repeats. The next human dies and the body is brought back to life and searches for another human to eat, around and around, until the human race is extinct. I would like everyone to know, after some investigating, at this point it doesn't seem like the Solis are leaving the cities yet. But it definitely appears they will be leaving soon, so we will have to discuss what we as a town are going to do. Part of tonight's agenda is to let you know what the elders have decided to do before the Solis inevitably reach our town." The room bursts into chaos and people scream over each other.

Nathan lets the unruliness continue to a crescendo and then smashes down his gavel furiously on the podium three more times. My father, who is next to him on ground level, shouts in his deep booming voice, "Silence! We will have order here or you will all be sent home!"

When my father shouts like this, there is no second-guessing him. Father constantly says what he means and means what he says, and the townspeople know it. Which was one of the reasons he was chosen as a town elder, his word could be trusted. One of the other reasons was he is a physically imposing man. He has a way of towering over everyone, even over people who are physically taller than him.

Over the years, a few people tried to take on my father and challenge his authority, but all it took was a few words from him and they would back down and submit with their tails tucked firmly between their legs.

In this moment, he is the leader and there is no saying otherwise. My father gazes up to Nathan and nods his head. "Nathan, the floor is yours again."

Nathan bows his head. "Thank you, Silas."

Nathan turns his attention back to the now quiet audience. "Now, as I was saying, the elders of our town have been throwing ideas back and forth over the past few days on how to combat this major crisis. Some of you may know there is a place called Sanctuary."

There is a mass intake of breath and Nathan holds his hand up to quiet the crowd. "We've scoured our old maps and think we know where Sanctuary is. There's a great crater in the world with what appears to be tunnels, which could hold a mass population of people underground, hidden from the rest of the world. We will be leaving to find Sanctuary and will take anyone who is willing to move there with us."

He rubs a hand over his face, the exhaustion clearly wearing him down. "Of course, no one is forcing you to uproot your lives and leave on this perilous journey with us, but in our opinion, this is the best choice for survival. The journey will take at least a week. Now, I know some of you have small children, but this is what the elders have decided is the best and safest way for everyone to go. We will be leaving in a week and a half, which should be plenty of time for those who wish to leave with us to get their affairs in order. Thank you for your patience." Without another word, Nathan turns and walks off the stage. Everyone in the great hall seems stunned for a moment, everything staying dead quiet, and then all hell breaks loose.

The townspeople start shouting. Some run towards the bottom of the stage to where my father is standing, yelling at him, asking what they should do. My father tries to stand his ground, but the crowd pushes him back against the stage and I can see that if this continues, things are not going to end well. I stand up from my seat and jump onto the stage where Nathan had been standing seconds before.

I call out, "Townspeople! I know we're all scared, and rightly so, but now is not the time to panic. Go home, get some rest, and let this sink in. Then you can reassess this news in a new light tomorrow."

A man who is standing next to my father and was seconds ago yelling and pushing him, stares me down with hatred in his dirt-colored eyes. The skin on his face is dark and almost scaly from being out in the sun too long. The years are etched clearly on his pompous face. His jowls droop and his gray straw-like hair caresses his small pencil-like shoulders.

"Why should we listen to a little girl like you Attina?" he seethes.

I turn my head to glower down at him and feel a strange, steadying warmth spread throughout my body. "Apparently, I'm the only one in here capable enough to not lose my shit." With a forcefulness in my voice I hadn't heard before, I growl, "Go home."

The man's eyes grow wide, and he hangs his head, defeated by my truth, and everyone starts calmly filing out of the building. My father gazes up to me with something close to admiration in his eyes. I smile down at him then stride around the podium and walk off the stage, but James has somehow pushed past everyone and is now on the stage next to me, standing right in my way.

A look of annoyance crosses his features. "Why did you get in the middle of it? You should've let the men take care of the situation. Girls shouldn't be spitting out orders."

His words are like a punch to the gut. "Well, asshole, I seemed to have diffused the situation even if I am only a lowly *girl*," I spit out.

The warmth I felt a second ago now leaves the rest of my body and zeros in on my palms. I rub my palms down my sides, silently reminding myself I shouldn't hit him. I spin on my heels and walk away from him without another word. His eyes follow me all the way to where my father is already standing at the other end of the hall.

I walk up to my father and wrap my arms around him. Just being in his presence calms me, and the heat and anger in me seeps away from my body. He's never made me feel like being a girl was a bad thing or that I was less important than a man. His sweet, woodsy smell fills my nostrils and I turn my head up to scan his face. He's worried, I can tell by the way his face sags at the corners. I give him a warm smile. "Let's go home."

Father smiles back down at me. "When did you get to be such an adult?" He searches my face for a second before continuing, "Yes, it has been a long day, pumpkin. Let's get some rest." His gaze travels up behind me. "Will you be walking home with us?" he asks who I presume to be James.

I cringe and turn to face James. He leers down at me with a strange glint in his eyes. "Of course, I'll be walking you both home. After this news, I don't want to be far away from our girl."

My father nods. "Good, I'm glad."

I roll my eyes and head for the door alone. Outside of the hall, I wait for Father and James to follow me. When they make it out, I loop my arm through my father's strong arm. No one says a word until we make it back to the house. There is too much on all of our minds for much discussion between the three of us. When we make it back to the cottage, Father invites James inside to sit down for some coffee.

Our small one-story log cottage isn't much, but it's home. My father built it when I was just a baby. The cottage has two bedrooms, a kitchen slash living room and a bathroom, which Father and I have day in and day out shared. After the town meeting, seeing my front door is a welcomed sight. All I want to do is to crawl into my soft bed and drift away to dreamland. As we all walk in the house, I announce I am going to bed and head to my room. Father nods his head and moves to the kitchen to start making coffee, but James grabs me by the arm as I move to walk down the hall.

He gazes at me with soft sad eyes. "Goodnight, Attina."

"Goodnight, *asshole*," I hiss, tearing my arm out of his hand as I head to my room.

When I reach my room, I change into my favorite nightgown and pull my blankets back and crawl into my plush straw and goose down bed. I lay in my bed for a long time thinking about what was said at the meeting tonight. I try to keep my mind on the fact that the Solis exist and what a shock this is for everyone, but my mind keeps traveling back to James and all the things we've gone through in the past few days.

Right when I'm about to fall to sleep, I hear a *clink clink* against the window behind my head. I stand up and pull back the same ugly beige window curtains I've had my entire life and jump back with a start. James's face is pressed up next to my window. Ugh, this is not what I wanted to deal with at the moment. He motions for me to open my window. Rolling my eyes, I open one of my windows, but only a crack.

"What do you want? I'm trying to sleep."

James clamors slightly up to my window and sticks his head through the crack. "Attina, can I come in?"

"No, James. I'm in bed, and you should do the same. It's been a long day," I spit out through gritted teeth.

I push on the window to try to close it, but he pushes violently back and slams my window open.

"Attina, I genuinely need to talk with you. Please let me in." Panic laces his voice.

I stare out the window at his face in the moonlight. Something about it seems different, broken almost. I open the other window and back up to give him room to crawl through. He awkwardly climbs into my room and walks over to me, wrapping his arms tightly around me. I let him hug me for a second, only because of how pitiful he's acting. Then I push him away.

"What do you want James? I don't really feel like being around you right now," I snap coldly.

James flinches like I've physically slapped him. "About earlier at the town meeting—" his voice cracks.

I hold my up hand to stop him. I'm too tired to have this conversation, and honestly, I'm still pissed about earlier. But, of course, he ignores me and pushes on.

"No, Attina. I need to get this off my chest. Today what I said, I didn't mean it. You are the most capable person I know. I lost my family all those years ago, but as soon as we met you became my new family, whether you know it or not. But you don't need a man in your life for you to be happy which scares me. The fact that you don't need me makes me feel useless, like I could disappear, and you wouldn't notice." As he finishes his appeal, he peeks back up at me searching my face for something. Acceptance maybe? Now I can see fear scrawled on his features. The look breaks me.

I instantly forgive him for any mean or rotten thing he's ever said to me in the past. I walk over to him and wrap my arms around him. "James, I will always need you. You are like family to me too. You disappearing would break me," I whisper, and I hug him as tightly as I can, hoping the force of my hug will help him realize he's not useless.

As the hug ends, he pulls me away from him an inch. His eyes meet mine like they're searching for an answer. Then, he leans in and kisses me slowly, tenderly. This is only our second real kiss. Over the years there have been a few stolen kisses between us, but those kisses were between children, this one means something more.

His lips are soft against mine, and there's a sense of urgency in his kiss. He pulls my body toward him tighter and wraps his arms around my waist while he urges my lips apart with his tongue. He starts walking me backwards until my thighs push against the side of my bed. His arms slowly move from my waist down to my thighs. He picks me up and lays me gently on the bed, his body following me until he is on top of me, owning my mouth. My heart races. Several conflicting emotions settle into my bones as we kiss. Whether I acknowledge it or not, I know he's right and we will end up together some day.

His mouth is hard on mine as I start unbuttoning his pants, but before I can get the first button undone, James stops and jerks away.

"No, not in your father's house. Not like this."

I gawk at him, embarrassed and angry. I can't believe I thought he wanted me. James must be able to read my thoughts because he stumbles, "Attina no! It's not like that! Trust me, I honestly would love to do this with you, but it's not the right time."

His words ease me, and I kiss him softly one last time, all the fire and anger instantly leaving me. "Then you should get going before we give in to temptation. We have to hunt tomorrow, so we could both use the rest."

He nods his head and retreats for the window, but I grab his thickly corded arm, my insecurity rearing its ugly head.

"Still meet you at the entrance at dawn?" I ask.

A smile slowly spreads across his face. His eyes light up and he lifts my hand to his lips, kissing it gently. He gazes up at me under his brows with his lips still touching my skin and whispers against my skin, "Always." Without another word, he pulls away and crawls out of my window disappearing into the night.

4

ATTINA

After James leaves, I crawl in bed and think over what happened today. It's a huge blow. I feel like the whole town kept so much from all of us who grew up here. The Solis are real? How is such a thing even possible? It's like they just told us the monster under the bed is real.

I think back to what I know about the Fae...

Even as a child I consciously knew they were out there—the Fae, the beings with magic flowing through them. Although I hadn't ever seen one for myself, I knew everything a human girl like me could know about them... or so I thought.

Growing up, all the children in our town were told stories about the Fae. I guess you could call them scary stories. Stories where a Fae drags a fair maiden back to its' realm and she doesn't ever return. What a simpler time when fairies were only characters in a story. These stories were even called fairytales. Those were the good ole days when the monsters weren't real; now it seems like they are.

These fairytales also came with a history lesson...one which I'd memorized by heart. It was the history of how humans and Fae became open enemies during The Day of Destruction. A day when one world crashed into another, when the age of man and metal relinquished its reign and the age of Fae and magic dominated. Magic, like all things, can bring light or dark into the world.

Preceding The Day of Destruction, fairies were thought of as something out of one's imagination, up until one rich, ignorant man decided to build a railroad line. This railroad line had to pass through a huge mountain, a mountain whose peak was so high it passed through the clouds. The mountain was named Shadow Mountain.

Shadow Mountain was covered in deep, dark, ancient forests full of strange creatures and archaic magic. Stories from the few people who survived entering that ancient magical forest said it was filled with deadly creatures, which couldn't be found anywhere else in the world. The floors were covered in so many tiny creatures, from ants to lizards, the floors seemed alive. If you didn't watch your step, it could be your last.

Only one Indian tribe was known to live in these conditions; somehow living harmoniously at the base of the mountain with the terrifying creatures inhabiting the forest. Creatures of such disarming beauty covered in scales and venom tipped wings, their bodies so iridescent and beautiful, it was hard to believe they could be so savage.

It's said men who wandered into the forest and ran into these creatures would be stopped cold in their tracks by the creature's beauty and by the time they realized they were the prey it was too late.

There were even rumors of flying bats bigger than a house and capable of eating a human whole. Even the ants crawling on the forest floor were deadly; if someone were unlucky enough to step on one barefoot, the ant's blood was poisonous enough to kill a child and make an adult violently ill. Still, Shadow Mountain stood between the old world and the new. The railroad would connect the previously built railroad tracks and the biggest town on the coast.

Being a man of destiny, the proprietor wanted more than anything to be remembered for changing the world. Many people told him of the dangers and pleaded with him to take the long way around the ancient mountain instead of blasting through it, but the proprietor wouldn't hear of it. Fears grew exponentially the closer the railroad came to the mountain.

The workers for the railroad were all average, poor men, but not stupid, and legends ran wild throughout their camp. Many of the workers grew up hearing stories of the beautiful creatures that inhabited the woods, but even worse were the stories of the people who lived underneath Shadow Mountain.

According to legend, an ancient race of mystical people lived under the mountain. It was said these people were twice the size of a normal human and had ragged, sharpened teeth which could rip out the throat of any man unlucky enough to fall into their clutches. The proprietor's advisers tried to talk some sense into him and ask him to simply go around the mountain instead of through it, but the proprietor would not listen.

He would scream at his advisers, "It will cost twice as much to skirt around that damned mountain you superstitious fools!"

"Sir, the workers are, and will be, scared out of their minds the whole time or we'll have a large number quit completely."

This didn't give him a second thought. "You idiots! Men

are a dime a dozen out there and I will not be bullied into this idea."

"We're not trying to bully you, sir, we're only trying to say, sometimes superstitions aren't simply superstitions, and leaving things we don't understand alone is sometimes the best option."

The proprietor wouldn't hear of it though, he just rolled his eyes, annoyed at the foolishness around him.

"My decision is final."

It was a decision he would regret for the rest of his life. Legends or no, the lure of the mountain was too strong for him to turn away or alter his path. He wanted to make it his prize conquest. The irony was the fact his greatest wish would come true, he would become a legend, just not the way he wanted to.

The Day of Destruction happened when the railroad builders used dynamite to blow a hole in the face of the mountain, all the way to its' heart. The day started off with three colossal booms followed by an ominous silence. Then all hell broke loose.

The chaos that ensued was as if the miners had opened up a door to the underworld itself, and once opened there was no escape. The Fae were everywhere in an instant. When the dust cleared, the massacre had already started. The Fae were slaughtering every single man in sight, like ghosts in the wind. There was no way the humans could defend against them; the Fae were incredibly strong and incredibly fast. After the melee had ended all the men, including the proprietor, had fallen.

For the Fae, blowing out the side of the mountain, and in turn their home, was an act of war. The Fae's goals from then on was to get back at humans, to repay them for blowing up their home by killing or enslaving every single human.

By the end of that infamous day, the age of man had also come to a conclusion, and a new age, the age of the Fae, had risen and would cover the world like the night itself.

After the Day of Destruction, it was like someone had knocked down an angry wasps' hive. Fae were everywhere around the world and humans had to scatter to stay alive. Some stayed hidden in the big cities, but most decided to move to small towns secluded from the rest of the world. Towns much like my own hometown.

Nowadays, I know humans aren't being actively hunted by the Fae anymore. From what Father has told me, one day the hunting suddenly stopped. They were hunting humans and taking them for slaves one day, and the next the Fae were nowhere to be seen. I hadn't even really thought about the Fae growing up. They were just some evil darkness in the world towering over us from afar. Now I know that isn't completely true, the darkness is a lot closer than I ever thought possible.

While the Fae might not be actively hunting humans for slaves anymore, they unleashed the Solis to kill and change each and every last remaining human. As I drift off to sleep, my last thoughts are of the realization that someone will have to stop the Fae before our species gets wiped out completely.

5

————

ATTINA

THE NEXT MORNING AT THE CRACK OF DAWN, I'M LOST IN thought as I walk to meet James at the town entrance. This morning the flying objects were worse. Instead of small objects floating around the room, I woke up to my desk chair whizzing erratically around my bed. I panicked again and sailed out of bed yanking the chair down as fast as I could, which seemed to fix the problem.

I'm starting to worry. Whatever this is, it's getting worse, not better. Before it was only the small, light objects in my room. I could deal with those things. Now whatever this is moving on to chairs? This can't be good news.

But even with all of this craziness going on, I woke up nervous for a completely different reason. I've been nervous since I opened my eyes this morning. I've been thinking over and over what happened last night between James and me. Will things be awkward between us?

I see him in the dewy morning light walking to the edge of town and my breath hitches. Today I see the light bouncing off his beautiful black hair, pulled back in a leather thong like usual. He walks up to me and without hesitation gives me a hug like he does each morning, but this time the hug is a little longer and a little deeper.

As we walk out of town, things between us are a little tenser, quieter, but after a few minutes together, everything goes back to normal, and I feel myself settling back into our normal routine.

The morning air is brisk and chilly against my skin. Clouds cover the sky, and the air smells heavy and sweet like it constantly does before it rains. As we walk out of town side by side, I peer up at James.

"It smells like rain."

"Yes, it does, we'll have to check the traps quickly if we don't want to get stuck in it. All the bigger game will be bedded down out of the rain, but we still need to find out if they're stocked for the townspeople." I nod and let James lead as we head to our first trap of the day.

It feels marvelous being out in nature. It's a calming sensation listening to the birds chirp and the leaves rustling together. Everything would be perfect if I didn't have James's eyes on me constantly.

The heat rises to my cheeks each time I notice him staring intently at me from his peripherals. I don't want to chase off any game around us so I whisper, "Why do you keep staring at me like that?"

"I'm just appreciating how completely gorgeous you are when you're in your element," he whispers back. The heat rises with a vengeance in my cheeks, shattering the calm feeling I had moments ago. James must see this happen because as soon as I glimpse away from him, he releases a deep chuckle.

We continue checking the traps one by one, until we finally make it to the last trap, which also happens to be the trap farthest from town. Today's haul has been meager at best. So far, we've only caught one squirrel, which is so skinny it can only be of use for its pelt, but today wasn't useless. The squirrel's pelt will be made into a fur muff or maybe fur socks for one of the kids in town to use during our cold winters.

Walking up to the last trap, I can already tell it'll be empty. I can see the sad, and empty loop we left yesterday. Something came and munched on our bait, but whatever it was it was smart because it hadn't set off the snare in the process. Leaving nothing but an empty trap.

"We'll just have to re-bait the snare and try again tomorrow."

I glance up at James as I bend down and re-bait the trap. When we make eye contact, I see all the love for me in his eyes, but there is also something else behind his stare. It's like his eyes and the rest of his face are telling two different stories. The tilt to his eyebrows and the almost snarl of his mouth makes him seem almost envious of me, but that can't be possible. Maybe what I'm seeing is more of a possessive expression? No that can't be, James wouldn't be envious or possessive of me. I shake myself out of those thoughts and continue my work on the snare.

"Well, today was a bust," I say, trying to clear the awkward tension in the air between us, but as I finish my sentence, I hear a branch snap behind us. We both spin around in surprise and I see a deer speeding away from us at a dead run. Without thinking, I whirl so I'm kneeling on one knee, pulling the bow off my back and knocking an arrow nearly simultaneously. My vision zeroes down to nothing but my target.

I can hear James snapping out something, but I can't make out his words, all I hear is my heart pounding, filling my chest. I pull back on my bow, the string groaning with protest. I have to pull the bowstring to its max. The deer is running fast and gaining more distance by the second.

My shot has to be perfect, and the deer is too far away for me to even be a hair off. I breathe in deeply, calming my racing heart, putting all my energy into this shot. The deer is out of range now, but I have to try. We provide food for the town and I don't want to head back with only a measly squirrel. A strange heat courses through my body spreading through my shoulders and arms, the warmth giving me confidence and reassuring me. I release the arrow and it soars through the air.

Thunk!

My arrow hits its mark, sinking deep into the deer's neck. The arrow hits the deer so violently, it trips and falls hard to the ground with a loud crash, breaking branches as its weight settles on the forest floor. I'm not sure how my arrow hit the deer with that kind of force when it was so far away, it shouldn't have been physically possible, but I don't care. I made the shot!

A big grin spreads across my face until I glance up at James's face. Immediately the grin disappears, and I regret my snap decision to fall the deer. His face shows disappointment. I thought he would be proud, since I made such an amazing and difficult shot, however, I see nothing but dismay written all over his face.

"Did you even think before you made that shot?" he snaps.

"What do you mean?" I say, taken aback.

"There's no way we'll have time to dress that deer before this rainstorm hits." His voice sounds frustrated and defeated as he grimaces and pinches the bridge of his nose between his fingers.

"I'm sorry. I didn't think... I just—" I stumble out, but the words are left on my lips when James turns around and walks off to the carcass calling over his shoulder.

"Let's get started, it's gonna to take a while to gut and quarter this thing."

Almost as soon as we finish gutting and quartering the deer the sky opens up and pours down on us, meaning we will have to stay out here until the rain clears. I carried the bow out here and James carried the machete and the satchel with our supplies for the day. In his bag we have a knife, ropes, water, a small first aid kit, and a canvas tent barely big enough for one person. Alas, this is an emergency and it'll have to do.

"Okay, I'll tress up the deer into that tree over there and you set up the tent here. I don't want you trekking through this rain and catching a cold, so we'll have to wait it out," he says with authority clear in his voice. There will be no second-guessing him this time. He hands me one of the smaller ropes and stalks away without a word.

Working through the rain is miserable. Everything becomes slippery and my fingers become numb and are like ice by the time I get the rope strung up between two big, strong oaks. I fold the canvas in thirds making sure to keep one side dry. Throwing over a third of the material on top of the strung rope, I am able to make a tent-like structure with a dry canvas floor to keep us off of the freezing, wet ground.

I crawl in and sit down, shuck off my wet shoes and socks, cross my legs, and wait. I feel like an errant child waiting to get a talking to for something she did wrong. What was I thinking? Why did I make that shot?

I think back to when I first saw the deer running. I remember feeling excited, but not for the kill like I thought it would be. No, I was excited to provide a good meal to the townspeople. I find it strange. I haven't ever felt like I was a real member of the community. I've only ever been an elder's daughter who was satisfactory at hunting.

Today though, I wanted to provide for everyone, take care of everyone like they were my responsibility. That shocks me. When did I start to care about these people? I mean I know they're the only people I've ever known my whole life but when did they become *my* responsibility? I think back over the past few days, what changed?

Last night, at the meeting, I saw everyone scared and shaken. Mothers were holding their crying children, men shielding their families like they could save them from the coming danger even now. That's when it happened, when I started to feel like these were my people. It's why I stood up last night to calm them, and why I didn't back down against such a boisterous man. They needed someone to be their rock, which I'd apparently decided to become.

Then James flings open the tent flap and barges in like a bull. He's drenched from head to toe in rain and sweat, but the odor coming off of him is still intoxicating. It's infuriating. James doesn't ever smell bad, the more he works, the better his aroma, like sweet cedar wood. I need to concentrate on the problem at hand, so I have to pull myself together and stop thinking of this man's scent.

"I don't regret killing the deer, it's for—" but I don't get to finish my thought. James leans in and puts his forefinger over my lips to quiet me.

"I know why you did it, which only makes me love you more."

His face is so close to mine, when he speaks, his sweet breath warms my face. I can almost breathe in the essence of him. Instantly, I have an overwhelming need to make his body a part of mine, which makes me feel powerful. In this moment, James is so masculine and all I want to do is make his masculinity a part of me. All of his male traits seem exaggerated and seeing him like this makes me tingly, like a lightning strike in my body is calling out to his body.

He leans down toward me, his big broad arms on either side of my body. His presence pushes me to lean back against the canvas. As he lumbers over me, his biceps ripple, and a growl slips out from his throat.

"I want you," he groans.

I open my mouth to answer but his lips cover mine before I can utter a word. The fervor coming off of him makes me melt into his kiss. All words are forgotten. A warmth flows through my body like liquid fire and I kiss him back hard, pulling his strong, muscled body on top of mine. His weight on me is comforting. I run my hands up and down his rock hard back, feeling the muscles ripple as he explores my body.

His fingers dig into my hips like claws claiming what's his. I reach under his shirt gently stripping him of the soaked garment. Our mouths separate for the few seconds it takes for me to pull his shirt over his head and for the first time since we started kissing, our eyes meet. His eyes shine with passion.

As soon as I get James's shirt over his head, his mouth is feverishly back on mine, claiming me. His hand begins roaming under my shirt. I press my body up into his hand. He pulls away, sitting back on his knees and lifts my wet shirt over my head taking a long hungry, hard stare at my half naked body. He growls, his need growing, as his hands reach down to my pants, ripping at the buttons like a lost man clawing at his salvation.

When I awaken, the rain has passed, and I'm left alone in the tent naked and cold. After we... I must've fallen asleep. Heat rises to my cheeks as I think back to what happened between us. I touch my lips and smile. A tingle of warmth resonates through me one more time. James throws open the tent door flaps. I flinch and unsuccessfully throw my arms around my body in an attempt to cover my bare body.

"Hey, it's clear now, we should get going."

I blush and nod my head in agreement. James runs his eyes freely over my body, almost hungrily. I scoff and roll my eyes. "I need to get dressed."

A wicked grin crosses his face. "I can wait." My jaw drops and I lean forward, and rip close the tent sides in his face. As I dress, his annoyed voice floats into the tent.

"Hurry up, we need the canvas to wrap the meat in."

As he finishes his sentence, I open the tent and walk out. "Quick enough for you?"

All of a sudden out of seemingly nowhere fear grips me hard in my belly. I fell asleep next to James. Did any objects move while I was asleep? If they did, did he see it? Should I bring it up? No, that would be a horrible idea. If nothing happened while I was sleeping, he'll just think I'm going crazy or something. Besides, he hasn't brought it up yet. Objects flying around a tent would definitely be the first thing he would talk to me about when I woke up. I hope I'm just being paranoid.

Pushing the worry in my head aside, I busy myself by breaking down the tent and using the canvas to wrap the deer meat in, strapping half of it on my back and half on James's back. Carrying this much weight is difficult for me but I bear through it because I know a hunter needs to be able to carry at least half of what they kill.

I'm so bogged down with all this extra weight and my

body is so exhausted from what James and I did, that as we head home it takes everything I have to put one foot in front of the other. As we walk back into town the sun is fading fast and a full moon is starting to rise. I'm beat and soaked to the bone from having the wet canvas strapped to my back the whole walk home. Right as we get to the edge of town, I drop the meat off my back and sit down. My body won't hold up to me taking one more step with an icicle frozen to my back.

James hadn't said much on the way back but when he sees me drop a warm smile crosses his face. He picks up my burden like it weighs nothing and says, "Why don't you head home and get warm? You must be drained. I'll handle this."

I don't waste a second before I jump up and give James the biggest hug I can muster and thank him before I run home to my warm bed. Father is not home by the time I make it back. Perfect, I won't have to explain my long absence. He must be talking with the other town elders about last night's meeting. I warm up some water, take the quickest bath of my life, change into clean, dry, warm clothes, and barely make it to bed before I quickly fall fast asleep.

6
____

JAMES

She's mine!

After what just happened between us, I know she's mine forever now.

All of my dreams have finally come true!

7

ATTINA

I WAKE UP THE NEXT MORNING TO THE SOUNDS OF BIRDS chirping and sunshine dancing across my tired eyes. It's strange waking up in such a normal way after my whole world's been turned upside down these past couple of days. I feel like everything I thought to be true was, in reality, a lie.

I sit up and study my room, but it's one of the only things that hasn't changed; everything is still in its place. My wooden nightstand with my favorite childhood stuffed animal in the middle is still there, and my matching wooden desk across the room with my favorite chair parked right next to it like usual.

That's when I realize it, nothing moved, which means nothing was flying around my room last night. Maybe whatever has been happening to me stopped? But why? This new development, along with everything else that has been happening in my life, leaves me more lost than ever.

After the past few nights, I don't know whom I can trust anymore. How had the entire town kept such a monumental secret all these years? How had my own father kept this secret from me this whole time? I never thought he would lie to me about something like this, but I guess I was wrong. Before I can even stand up out of bed, my father opens the door. Unlike his usual dignified clothes, today he is wearing dark leathers. I've never seen him wear this type of clothing before, so I'm intrigued.

"Hey, pumpkin."

His face is expectant and there is something strange in the tone of his voice, but even after keeping such a huge secret, I'm pleasantly surprised to realize I still completely trust him. In my heart, I know he thought he was protecting me from the worry and the stress this new knowledge would cause me.

I sit up and stare at him. I'm extremely curious what this could be about. He plops down on the foot of my bed, his face looking solemn. He takes a long, deep breath like he is trying to fortify himself for whatever he's about to say.

"Attina, we need to talk. You're old enough now, and after such a world shattering town meeting you need to know some things."

When his words settle over me, I feel myself jerk, I don't know if I can take any more surprises, but for him I will try. I gaze at him with questioning eyes. "I'm all ears."

He reaches out his hand and covers my ankle with it. His hand is warm and steady like it's been my entire life without fail. Growing up without a mother was hard, but having his shoulder to cry on made it a little bit easier. He's my rock, plain and simple.

His hand tightens on my ankle for a second and then I notice he's shaking his head, "No, pumpkin, I don't want to do this here. I've been thinking, and I've decided it's best if we have a daddy daughter camping week like we used to do when you were little. I have all my stuff packed up to go and the horses are saddled already."

That shakes me. My whole life he's always asked my opinion on big things like this, and he hasn't forced me to do anything since I'd become a teenager. My shock must be written all over my face, because after a second he says, "I know I'm throwing all this on you at once and it must seem like I'm pressing this on you, but please could you do this one thing for me? It would mean a lot to your old pops."

He's perpetually been an extremely quiet, stoic person, so this plea chops down the anger swelling in my stomach before it can truly manifest. I plaster a forced smile on my face.

"Yes, of course I will go with you."

I'm worried about what he could possibly have to tell me which would require such a trip. I haven't ever seen him with this kind of worry in his eyes, but I keep my smile painted on my face anyway.

At hearing my answer, he smiles, nods his head and walks out of my room. I get dressed quickly. It's only the beginning of spring and still cold, so I put on some warm shoes, a warm jacket, and pack my saddle-bag full of clothes and necessities, then walk to the backyard where our horses are stabled.

Our horses, Oak and Raven, are already tied to a hitching post behind our house. Like Father said, both horses are all saddled and packed for a long haul.

I walk up to Oak and rest my palm on his warm neck, whispering, "Hey, old man."

Oak has been my horse for as long as I can remember. He is tall, buff, and a deep creamy yellow color. His mane and tail are a shiny and dark black, so black it seems to swallow up all the other colors around it. But his eyes are the most beautiful thing about him. They are full of every single color I can imagine, making them appear as if they are starlight.

He's the most level-headed horse I've ever ridden in my life. Nothing's ever spooked him, and he's constantly made taking care of me his first priority. Growing up, I'd been sort of a wild child, getting Oak and myself into some crazy and dangerous situations, and he always made sure we made it out together.

Raven, on the other hand, is a different story. Raven is a younger mare and we basically grew up together. When I was born, she was a wild free spirited two-year-old. From as far back as I can remember she had a fiery, ornery personality.

Father told me when she was younger it was like she'd refused to be tamed; he'd admired her for her fire. Father worked tirelessly for years with her and eventually, they learned to trust each other and become partners. Raven was, and is still, no horse to be submissive. She became my father's partner because she wanted to be, and *only* because she wanted to be. If anyone else tried to ride her, she would buck them off as soon as their butt hit the saddle. I'd seen it myself when Nathan tried to ride her once many years ago.

She's the strongest willed horse I've ever met in my life. She is a stout, powerful, dark blood bay mare. Her color is like someone took a bucket full of blood and painted her with it. Her mane and tail are so black they almost appear blue and to top it all off she has the lightest gray eyes, which remind me of the color of fog in the early morning. She is a stunning horse to behold.

For my Father though, she is a miracle. She has so much heart for him. I truly believe she would do anything for him. If he asked her, I know Raven would pull twice her body weight to please him.

Once, years ago, Oak and I had been on an all-day winter trail ride, which ended with both of us falling through an iced over lake.

After a long day of exploring, I suddenly realized it was much later than I'd thought, and we were going to be late getting home. Growing up, whenever I was late getting home, Father wouldn't yell at me, he would talk to me, for hours. We would sit down at the dinner table and he would ask me over and over why I was late and did I know how it made him feel. He would lay out each and every scenario of what could've happened to me, which his worried imagination had spit out. Getting yelled at would've been much easier to deal with, there was no way I was going to be late coming home, so I hatched an insane plan.

On our ride that morning, Oak and I had gone the long way around a frozen lake; it had taken a few hours to go around it, which was fine. We'd had all day to do it at the time, but the way back home was a different story. The sun was setting, and we needed to make it back home before dark unless I wanted to go through one of those famous talks. So, I decided we would just try to skirt around the lake.

The worst part was the lake was at the bottom of a sheer rock cliff, so there weren't many options on how to get past it, only by traversing a narrow trail between the cliff and lake. We started on the trail and made it halfway around the lake before it happened. The trail eroded under our combined weight and we tumbled down to the lake, the thin ice giving way.

It was the single most terrifying moment of my life. The frigid water was lapping over my head. Somehow, I was able to find Oak in the freezing water and grab back onto his saddle. As soon as he felt my weight back on top of him, he got his feet under him and was able to pull us out of the ice, and in some kind of miracle, he was able to shoot up the side of the cliff. Something no normal horse should have been physically capable of doing after a fall like that.

Once we topped the precipice, he took off like a shot towards home. He raced all the way home pushing his frozen body to its max. When we made it to my back door, I was able to fall off of Oak and drag myself to the back door. I remember Oak loudly whinnying and then nothing. When I woke up again, I was laying in front of our lit fireplace where Father must have carried me.

I could have died that day, but Oak took care of me. Needless to say, I trust him with my life.

Father didn't tell me our horses were Fae horses until after the fateful day in the frozen lake. Up until then, the horses were not allowed to talk around me, but afterwards, Father thought it better to finally tell me the truth. Growing up, the only horses I was ever exposed to were Oak and Raven, so I didn't realize there was something different about them.

They of course listened to my physical commands, but also listened to my vocal commands. They rarely spooked and never bucked with me on their backs. I barely remember when my father first mentioned the horses talking. It was right after Father found me freezing and as he was warming me up, he kept mumbling to himself over and over, "I should have just told her..."

When I woke from my coma later in the night, or what I thought was a coma, the first words out of my mouth were, "What should you have told me?"

By now I was in bed, and Father was sitting at my bedside. His hair was a mess, probably from dragging his hands through it throughout the night. His eyes were bloodshot from crying, or lack of sleep, I'm not sure. At the sound of my voice, his head turned to me, and I could see he had a dreadful expression on his face, his eyebrows are drawn, and his lips pursed, like he'd seen a ghost.

"I should've told you the horses could talk. I was wrong to think you were too young and couldn't keep a secret, but maybe if I had told you, then Oak could have talked you out of taking such a risky shortcut and could have prevented this accident."

I was floored. Father went on to tell me Oak and Raven were Fae horses and they could talk and had a few other powers. That was all I would get out of him though. He smiled and told me I would find out all I wanted to know later, and rubbed my head, told me I needed rest, and put me to bed. I was exhausted, so I didn't fight him on it, and we didn't really ever talk about it again.

My father had been the one to tell me about our Fae horses and I trusted him implicitly, so there hadn't been a need for more talk on the subject. I also knew anything associated with the Fae wouldn't be seen in a favorable light in town, so I knew this was something not to be spoken of with others, not even James.

8

ATTINA

I TIE MY SADDLE BAG, FILLED WITH MY CLOTHES AND necessities for the trip, to Oak's saddle and haul myself on top of him. When I get settled into my saddle, I reach down to pet his neck.

"Are you ready for another adventure old man?" Oak turns his head towards me and bows his head.

"Yes, my lady."

Ever since I had found out our horses could talk, Oak would call me "my lady". I'm not sure why he does it. It's not like I asked him to. By no means have I ever felt like a lady.

My father walks out of the back of our house and for the first time he looks old to me. Today I can see the years weighing on him, and it seems like he has added ten years to his life overnight. His face seems haggard and limp and somehow his hair even looks grayer to me.

With his head down, he walks over to Raven and ties his last pack to her, making sure each pack is balanced perfectly to ease the burden. As soon as father has checked both horses' packs, he glances back at me with something akin to sorrow in his eyes.

"Are you ready, pumpkin?" he asks with a sad voice.

His broken tone shocks me so much I feel my breath catch, and I can only give him a curt nod. Raven then knickers at my father and for the first time in Raven's life he doesn't pat her in acknowledgement. Something must be tremendously wrong if father is too caught up in his own thoughts to acknowledge his horse.

The trip to our yearly camping grounds is a slow trek this time. The horses are weighed down heavily, which means we will probably be camping for more than a week. I know the town is leaving in two weeks, but I trust father and I know he has a plan to get us back to town on time. With all the extra weight, a trip which would've normally taken us about a day, takes three days instead.

Each and every year, Father and I would travel out to this same spot with Oak and Raven, only the four of us. We would leave town and all our responsibilities for a long weekend, spending our time fishing, hiking, and unwinding. I learned so much on these trips over the years; how to set up a tent, how to gut any animal, how to start a fire, and so much more. They were some of the happiest times in my life.

Our camping grounds are one of the most beautiful places I've ever seen in my entire life and I'm constantly so taken aback by its grace and peacefulness. We've been riding through the forest for days, so walking up to the meadow clearing we use as a campsite is a sight for sore eyes.

As we walk into the round, green, spacious clearing, I take a scan of the area. Surrounding the clearing on three sides is the lush, thick forest we've been riding in for days. A large knoll is hugged up against the last side. Running along the bottom edge of the knoll is a creek which curves and sways with the rolling hill.

The creek is the thing that makes this the perfect spot for camping. It makes for a short walk to get water for the horses and us. The creek also happens to have the added bonus of being brimming with fish each spring. Camping here always makes me feel happy and whole. My father told me when I was younger he and mother found this spot together shortly after they got married.

As soon as we enter the clearing, father gets off Raven, and without a word, starts putting camp together. He's in an ominous mood, so I start working to get camp set up too. I begin untacking the horses and getting a fire started since the sun is starting to set.

Nothing is said between us until camp is completely set up and we have some fresh fish cooking on the fire. Our fire is built in the center of our little camp and we have two rotted out logs on either side, which we use for chairs. Finally, my father gazes at me from across the fire. It seems like the first time in days he's actually seen me.

He clears his throat. "There are a few things I need to get off my chest and you are old enough now to know the truth. You've found out about the Solis and there is no way the timing of this is a coincidence. I have some things I need to tell you about your mother. First and foremost, your mother was Fae."

My jaw drops. Over the years, I've asked my father incessantly about my mother, trying to cling to any little piece of information about the woman who gave birth to me. All Father would ever tell me is I am the spitting image of her from my beauty to my personality. She had my same long, brown flowing hair. We have the same hourglass figure, but where my eyes are lightening blue like his, hers were fiery.

I'm not sure what color fiery is but it's how he's habitually described them.

The only other things he would tell me was that she was brave, fierce, a force to be reckoned with, and she died not long after giving birth to me. Anytime I asked for more information, he would get tears in his eyes and tell me it was too painful for him to talk about her. Now he's telling me I'm half Fae?

He pushes on. "Attina, I know I haven't ever told you enough about your mother, but you must've figured out by now I was protecting you by keeping the truth from you."

"Protecting me from what?"

His face falls, he stares down at the ground, and his shoulders drawn in on themselves. The air radiating from him is grave and uncertain. His voice becomes shaky. I haven't ever heard his voice crack out of him in such a trembling way before. He clears his throat.

"Your grandfather—"

"I don't have a grandfather. Your father died when you were a small boy and you told me my mother's father was non-existent in her life. I would assume by now he would have passed away anyway." Even as the words leave my mouth, I realize if he is Fae then it's possible he has a much longer lifespan than a human would.

My father averts his eyes and stares deeply into the fire between us. In them I notice the nervousness has left. Now I can see an extreme anger rising, and something I haven't seen before; an intense, burning inferno blazing hotter than the fire we're sitting by, the fire of death and destruction.

I perch there on my log across from him quietly, waiting for him to compose himself. He stays quiet for longer than I thought possible. When the quiet intensity becomes almost too much, he finally glowers back at me, but the anger in his eyes leaves a trace of sadness.

"No Attina, your mother's father, Henrik, is alive. And if he ever finds you, he will kill you." I suck in a sharp breath. My vision goes black for a second and a coldness, which wasn't there before, seeps into my bones.

"Wait. Henrik? Like the Henrik—"

"Yes, the same Henrik that Nathan talked about at the town meeting. Seeing the look on your face, I can tell by just hearing his name again, I know you can feel what he is— pure evil."

My father says the words with a horrifying coldness, and his shoulders slump forward like a weight has literally been taken off them. My eyes shoot to his dark and now menacing face.

I purse my lips and my jaw ticks. There are hundreds of questions begging to escape my lips, but before I can voice them, Father clears his throat. He lifts his hand and puts one finger up, silently asking me to give him a second to talk.

"Before you ask all the questions which are obviously bubbling out of you, let me explain who your mother actually was." He takes a deep breath before continuing.

"First off, your mother didn't die giving birth to you. She had to leave us for our safety. Your mother was the princess of the Fae world, the next in line for the throne, but she wasn't simply a princess. She was the fiercest, most feared warrior in her realm. She even became the King's personal slayer. Titania was your mother's given name, but I always called her my darling."

"Before I continue, I want to tell you your mother was an amazing, wonderful person. You remind me a lot of her actually. She was compassionate, caring, sweet and funny but could also take care of herself in any situation. Your mother was a total badass who had the biggest heart out of anyone I've ever met."

My brows raise and I shake my head. I lick my chapped lips and interrupt him. "Why did she abandon us then if she was as you say? How could she leave someone she supposedly loved and a newborn baby if she had such a big heart?" I swallow the giant lump in my throat as tears threaten to spill into a heavy downpour.

"Pumpkin, she never wanted to leave us. She was forced to leave. We weren't supposed to fall in love. She should've killed me on the Day of Destruction, but it was love at first sight and she left everything and everyone to be with me. She left the life she knew, her people and her responsibility. Then you came along, and our life was perfect. We were happy. Until the day her father found us."

"Henrik sent his own Fae soldiers to find her. He didn't know about the two of us, he only knew she had shirked her responsibilities and he sent those soldiers to bring her back to him." At this memory he takes in a shuddering breath and blows out the air slowly like he's trying to steady himself.

"You were in your mother's arms when her own soldiers and friends came for her. All three of us were sitting in our cottage around the fireplace relaxing before bed when the door burst open. She shielded you with her body and when the dust settled, we saw five soldiers blocking the only way out of our cottage. Titania handed you over to me as she spoke to her soldiers. She told them she couldn't allow them to live and report back to the King, so she took them on one by one. When all was said and done, she'd killed five of her soldiers and came out of it with a nasty gash across her chest. When she came back into the hut she was crying, but not from pain. She told me she had to leave. She had to keep us safe and the only way for her to do so was to head back to the king and her people. She said she would end that life and return to us, but the only way to keep us safe was to kill Henrik before he found out about you and me. Your mother promised to return as soon as the deed was done, but she never came back. I can only guess she lost in the fight against her father. Before she left though, she wrote a letter to you for when you got older, in case she wasn't able to return. I have her letter and I want you to read it."

I am completely speechless. This is too much information to process. I have no idea where to start. Father stands up and walks over to his saddle bag where he pulls out a piece of parchment with long, gracefully flowing and sparkling writing across it. He hands me the letter.

"Your mother wrote this in Fae ink, magic ink, which she spelled so only you could read the contents. I only know the general gist of what's in it."

I take the parchment in my hands. It's absolutely gorgeous, an off-white color with the texture of leather and dark blue ink sparkling in the light of the fire.

"Now, pumpkin, I'm going to hit the hay and give you some privacy. I want you to take as long as you need to read the letter and then get some rest. If you need me, just yell. Tomorrow we will start your training, so you'll need your rest".

"What training?" I burst out.

"It's all in the letter." He smiles down at me.

"Is that why you've been wearing those weird leather clothes?"

"Yes, they're fighting leathers." He rolls his eyes and laughs. "Just read the letter."

I stand up and walk over to Father and give him a big hug.

"Thank you for letting me know about Mother."

He hugs me back then pulls away and messes my hair. "Of course, pumpkin, I'm so sorry it took me too long to tell you all this." He rubs a hand over his face. "It's hard for me to talk about her."

I nod. "I understand."

After Father disappears into his tent, I sit back on my log holding the letter in my hands and stare at it. This contains the only words my mother has ever said to me. The realization makes my hands shake and I take a long, deep breath. The pungent, woody, sweet smell fills my lungs. I steel my nerves and slowly open the parchment.

Dear Attina,

If you are reading this, then I must be gone. Let me say first I am so sorry, baby girl. I never would have left you and your father if this wasn't the only way to keep you safe.

My father, the Fae King, is an extremely controlling and evil man, and if he ever found out about you or your father, he would kill you both, and I would rather die than see that happen.

I know this is difficult to understand at the moment, but if your father is giving you this letter, it is because your grandfather or his Solis are becoming a threat and your life is in danger.

Be a good girl and listen to your father. Everything he tells you is true. I am Fae, which means you are half Fae. I know you probably hate the Fae by now, but don't let your hatred of Fae seep into a hatred of yourself. If you are anything like me, or your father, you are smart, tough, and resilient. Use this to your advantage.

Your grandfather is the king of all the Fae. Which wasn't always the case. He is vile and a trickster, he will use any form of deception to achieve his goals. Those goals are to rule all of

Arealea. He took over both Fae kingdoms (West and East) at a young age through deception and trickery, so don't let your guard down when it comes to him.

The Day of Destruction was the excuse he needed to get the royal Fae families to agree to go to war for him against the humans he wanted enslaved. Once he has all the humans as slaves, or turned into one of his monsters, he will be the sole ruler of Arealea, and he will unleash a darkness, which no one will be able to escape. You cannot let his darkness consume the world.

Silas will teach you everything I taught him about being a slayer. You will need those skills to overthrow your grandfather and take your rightful place on the Fae throne.

Baby girl, you are human and Fae. You are the only one of your kind I know of in the world. This also makes you the only one who can sway the hearts and minds of humans and Fae alike. You are the best of both worlds and Arealea's only chance to finally unite everyone.

I am so sorry I won't be there to help you through your Awakening when your magic appears. The best advice I can give you is to listen to your body, and if all else fails ask your father or Oak what to do. They are there to support you, use them for guidance.

Most of all though, I am so sorry I didn't get to see you grow up. I would give anything to see your first steps, hear your first words, and help you navigate through your life. I love you more than the moon and stars, my baby girl.

Love forever and always,

Mom

P.S.

. . .

You are the true heir to the Fae throne. Don't ever forget that. I know you hate the Fae, but someday you will have to come to terms with who you are and reconcile your feelings over your people and yourself. I say your people, because that is exactly what they are. All the Fae are your people and your responsibility, Princess Attina.

Your father will teach you everything you need to know to take back your kingdom. Do what I could not and take down my father and save our people. Become the queen I could not.

Queen Attina?

My parents seriously expect me to kill my grandfather and become a queen? How is such a thing even possible? I can't even begin to wrap my mind around all of this.

9

ATTINA

TODAY IS TO BE OUR FIRST TRAINING SESSION. I HAD A FITFUL night's sleep thinking of everything Father told me last night. Reading the only letter my mother had ever written me and what Father is going to teach me today, kept my mind racing. Mother was a Fae princess. Does that make me a princess too? Even though I'm only half Fae?

I'd grown up hating the Fae for appearing on that fateful night and destroying our world. Father said the three of us had moved to the middle of nowhere to hide from the Fae and the Solis. What would life have been like without the Fae? What would life have been like if we'd lived with the Fae? What am I thinking, such a thing couldn't ever happen? A half-breed like me would never be welcome, and they would probably enslave Father. But what could have been didn't matter anymore. The Fae and Solis were a part of our lives and there's no way it would be changing anytime soon.

I don't know if I'll ever be able to live up to my parents' wishes. I agree I need to learn to protect my loved ones and myself, but I have no clue if I will ever be up to the task of taking over an entire kingdom. My mother was the greatest slayer in the Fae world and she obviously had failed against Henrik. She was a trained slayer, not a nobody like me. How could I ever dream of having a chance against someone like him?

Thankfully, she'd taught my father everything she knew. I can only guess she knew they wouldn't ever be safe, so she wanted him to survive any attack even if she wasn't there to protect him.

The first thing I see when I climb out of my canvas tent is a round clearing in the grass behind our campsite, which wasn't there last night. Father must have gotten up at the crack of dawn to knock down the tall grass covering the ground to clear this space.

I focus my gaze over to where Oak and Raven are happily eating by the creek. When they see me regarding them they glance between each other and seem to arrive at a joint decision. Oak lifts his gorgeous yellow, buckskin colored head.

"You will do great."

Then Raven's dainty, red head jerks to the side and she snaps at him, "Don't lie to her! Girl, you will never be as strong, cunning, swift, and fierce as your mother, so don't even try to be. Just try to learn enough to keep yourself from getting killed." This was typical Raven, we'd consistently had a love hate relationship over the years.

"Thanks for the vote of confidence, Raven." I retort, rolling my eyes. "At least now I know which horse is getting apples tonight." I wink at Oak. Raven can underestimate me all she wants, but I know in my heart I will become something special.

As I walk into the circular clearing, I spot Father, holding a pile of split wood, walking out of the tree line toward camp. When he sees me, he nods his head.

"Well, I'm glad that'll be my last load of firewood."

I stare at him confused. His blue eyes sparkle with amusement, the laugh lines around his eyes crinkling. "From now on, as part of your training, you will get up before dawn and gather and split the wood we will need for the day."

I whimper. "But, Father! Chopping wood has absolutely nothing to do with training! I want to train like a real warrior, like Mother!"

My father's smirk doesn't falter. "This is how real warriors are trained, you must first learn discipline, and only then will you begin to understand what a real warrior is. Now Attina, get your ass in that circle while I stack these logs by the fire."

His statement shocks me about as much as when I learned my mother was Fae. My Father didn't ever cuss, especially at me. The last time he'd cussed at me was a few days after Oak and I had almost frozen to death from falling through the ice. Back then, he'd wanted to have one of his talks and find out what was running through my head to go home the way I did. The last thing I want is to get a talking to like that again, so I move quickly to the clearing and wait.

As he joins me, he must see the shock written on my face. "What's wrong?"

I gulp and say meekly, "You never cuss. What did I do wrong?"

His brows scrunch and it appears like there is an inner conflict going on behind those aquamarine eyes of his. "I just want you to realize how serious this whole thing is. This isn't some game. You seem to think being a warrior is some noble privilege."

"Of course, it's a noble privilege!" I shout at Father, stunned. What is he talking about? I glance at him, feeling the confusion spread across my face.

He drops his head, draws a heavy sigh, closes his eyes, and pinches the bridge of his nose. Then he takes in a deep breath and releases it slowly before fixing his gaze back on me.

"You know, I once asked your mother why she became a slayer. I thought the same as you back then, it must be some high honor. Being a slayer sounds almost romantic, saving people from the big bad wolf kind of thing. Well, after your mother was done smacking me around a little bit," he says this with a slight smile and chuckle like it's a happy memory, "she explained to me why she chose to become a slayer."

I sit down on the soft green ground and gape up to my father in awe.

"You see, pumpkin, in the Fae world, a princess, especially the heir to the throne, is seen as someone who wears pretty dresses and throws extravagant parties. Frankly, in Fae royalty, women don't matter much. They are only thought of as the propionate of the race and nothing else. Such a lifestyle was not for your mother."

I am completely in rapture at this story already. My entire life I've known nothing about my mother, now that Father's willing to tell me things I find myself holding onto every piece of new information like they're pieces of some precious jewel.

"Growing up, your mother was not watched well by her handmaidens and she regularly snuck out of the castle to play soldier with her father's elite guard. She started learning to fight at a young age and fell in love with it. Day and night, she would work with the soldiers. Her father, Henrik, didn't care what she did with her time, as long as she fulfilled her duties of producing an heir when the time came, so at the age of thirteen she joined her father's elite guard and quickly ascended the ranks. When she turned sixteen, her father waged war on the Eastern Fae. At the time, Henrik was acting king because his father was elderly and not interested in being king anymore. This war was the first time your mother seriously saw how power hungry her father was."

I feel my eyes widen."Why did he the war?"

"He had absolutely no reason to start a war with the Eastern Fae. There were no political tensions, no threats, nothing. He simply wanted power. Henrik wanted to not only be acting king of the Western Fae, but he also wanted to be King of all the Fae. Being the only heir to the Western Fae throne, your mother was not allowed to join her soldiers in the battle." At this my father smiles and chuckles. "Knowing her though, I bet she put up one helluva fight to leave with them."

"Well did she go?"

"No, all she could do was sit by and watch as her only friends marched off to war without her. Many of her friends and soldiers did not make it back home. She always blamed herself for their deaths. Maybe if she was there, some of her friends would've made it home to their families."

I glare down at the ground, "how sad I can't imagine being able to get through that kind of pain."

"Yes Pumpkin, it is sad. From then on she decided she would protect all of her people at any cost. Her body and soul was no longer her own, but her people's. She threw herself into her training, learning everything she could from all the masters she could find. She learned about how to become a slayer by mastering poisons, stealth, strategy, and her own powers. Before she knew it, she was the best soldier in her father's elite guard. She thought if she was a perfect enough warrior, or a perfect enough slayer, she could protect her people. No more wars would be needed and no more of her people's lives would be lost. She'd give her father whatever kingdom he wanted on her own. You see pumpkin, your mother didn't become a slayer out of some noble privilege, she became a slayer to protect her people with every ounce of her being and every drop of her blood." At this Father sweeps his eyes across me. "Now it's your turn to pick up her responsibility. First for *your* people, and then for your mother's people."

I jump out of my sitting position and screech "They are the enemy!"

Father's eyes grow steely "No, they are not."

He shakes his head. "They are innocent. Your grandfather, Henrik, is the enemy. The Fae move on his orders—and his orders alone—and anyone who dares goes against the king's wishes meets a painful end. They are who your mother sacrificed everything for. They are your mother's people, and they are your people. You are part Fae and the only heir to the throne. The Fae people need you, they may not know it yet, but they need you to lead them."

As soon as the words leave his mouth, he throws a hard punch right into my gut. Instantly, all the air flies out of my body, my legs buckle, and I fall to the ground gulping to get air back into my lungs. The world tilts and black spots sparkle in my vision.

When I can breathe semi normally again and the world stops spinning I furrow my brows, harden my eyes, and give him a harsh glare. "What the hell? Why would you do that?"

Father gazes down on me sprawled in the grass with fire in his eyes as he circles me like a predator. "If you're going to be a leader, then you're going to have to be a helluva lot tougher than that, Attina."

"You snuck up on me! We were in the middle of a conversation! I'm plenty strong, but you didn't fight fair. You cheated!" I snap as I sit up.

Father glares at me with disbelief written on his face. "You honestly think someone who's trying to kill you will fight fair? I know I raised you smarter than that."

His answer infuriates me. How could he say such a thing to me? "Of course I don't think the enemy will fight fair, but I would assume you'd fight fair considering I'm your daughter." I stand up and brush myself off.

Father chuckles. "I can't fight fair if I'm going to prepare you for the future. Assume nothing, and trust no one. I'm not your friend while we're training. I'm going to get you prepared to defend yourself and to do so, I have to be hard on you." At this point his voice drops an octave lower. "Now get up and for mouthing off you can do fifty pushups."

Who knew stupid pushups could be this hard? I'd watched James do them before when he was trying to show off, but he always made them seem so easy. When I finish my pushups I thank the Gods I can finally rest my arms, but the thought quickly leaves my mind when I check around for Father. I glance all over camp and surprisingly it's empty.

When I open his tent flap I see nothing but an empty bed roll. Maybe the horses have seen him? I call out to Oak who's eating on the right hand side of camp, "Hey. Have you seen Father?" Oak lifts his head and shakes it at me.

Well, if Oak hasn't seen him, then he couldn't have gone

passed him, Oak would have noticed Father. The only other way he could have gone is to the left, past camp, but there's nothing that way, only the creek and the forest.

"Feel like helping me search for him, buddy?"

"Sure my lady," Oak responds happily as he trots over to me.

"Oh thank goodness." I sigh. "I'm sore from sparring. I could use another set of legs."

"He worked you over pretty hard didn't he?" He chuckles as he kneels down, making it easier for me to mount him.

"Yeah he did and then he just disappeared," I say as I climb on him bareback.

"Well, let's go find him," he responds as we trot off in search of Father

After a little while, we hear a thwack thwack noise. Like someone is chopping wood. Is he chopping wood? I thought that was my job? Besides, why is Father out here so far from camp?

Oak and I wander through the forest trying to pinpoint where the noise is coming from. We follow the sound until we run into the creek. From our vantage point we see Father across the creek, a sword in his hands slicing through an invisible opponent and striking his sword into a tree.

"Father!" I yell across the creek. He stops his ghostly fight and turns towards us.

"Hey guys." He lowers his sword and waves. "Oak, you can head back to camp. Attina, get over here." He gestures with his hand.

I jump off of Oak and walk up to his face. I wrap my arms around his massive head and nuzzle my face into the top of his head.

"I love you, old man. I'll see you later," I whisper to him.

"I love you too. Try to take it easy on him," He winks at me, then turns around, and starts his trek back to camp.

I turn and call out to Father, "Hey how do I get over there?"

No answer.

"*Hello?* Can you hear me?"

No answer.

He must be too far away to hear me now. I search to my left and my right. Down to the right are a few rocks, but the rocks are wet and might be slippery. I scan around again, but no other way to cross jumps out at me. I guess I have to cross over the rocks and hope I don't slip.

Walking up to the edge of the creek, I can see three rocks, which stand between the opposite bank and me. They're spaced out pretty evenly, but the water is lapping up over the top of them making them wet and a tad slimy. I take a big, long step out to the first rock, my boot gripping easily. The rock is only big enough for one foot at a time so my next step is to the second rock. It's not until I'm taking the step to the last rock that I know everything is everything is going to go terribly wrong.

It happens in slow motion. I take the step to the third rock and as I'm starting to put weight on the new rock, the foot on the rock behind me slips right out from under me. There's no way for me to catch myself and I fall down into the water, straight onto my butt. Being a klutz I've learned falling on your face hurts way too much. So over the years I've learned how to always fall on my butt. Somehow I get a mouthful of water and I end up chest deep in freezing cold water. My father appears on the other bank of the creek cackling.

He's doubled over at the waist, hands on his knees, laughing.

I stand up. "You know, you could be offering some kind of help instead of laughing your ass off at me," I snap in annoyance, but I'm also holding back a laugh myself. What can I say? His laughter is contagious. Before I know it, I'm laughing as hard as he is. I clamber out of the cold stream as I begin to get my chortling under control.

"Okay, if that's not the way you got over here, then how did you do it?"

Father puts his hand to my back and guides me farther down the creek. We walk around a bend in the creek. I hadn't bothered walking around it because I assumed Father hadn't gone this far out of his way.

When we get around the bend I see it, a downed tree stretching across the creek, it's big, and strong enough to cross over the water on foot. Father places his hand on my shoulder and turns me towards him.

"Pumpkin, you should remember you have to scout your surroundings at all times. It would have only taken you a few more minutes to find this and you would be dry right now instead of sopping wet. If you were in a battle, the few minutes it would've taken you to scout the area could mean the difference between life and death.

I let that sink in. I was careless. He's right, there's so much riding on me staying alive. There are people counting on me now, I need to be more careful. Even something so small and innocuous could mean life or death for more than just me now.

Father wraps me in a huge hug, sheaths his sword, and smiles as he pushes me away at arm's length. "Why don't we head back to camp and get you into some dry clothes before you catch a cold."

As we walk back to camp, I remember I had a question for him yesterday I didn't get a chance to ask.

"Um...Father...I have a question for you. I meant to ask you about it yesterday, but I forgot."

"Go ahead, pumpkin."

"In my mother's letter she told me to listen to my body when I come into my magic. What does that mean?" I try to keep the panic out of my voice. I know in my bones this magic has something to do with all the objects flying around in my room in my sleep.

He stops and turns around towards me placing his hand on my shoulder. "I don't know how I forgot to tell you this earlier. When a Fae grows up, their magic is awakened."

He pauses and squeezes my shoulder like it explains everything. "Now with you being half Fae, I'm not sure if you'll even have powers or how they will manifest, but I will help you navigate through them if they show up."

"So, would objects flying around my bed while I sleep count as powers?" I timidly ask. I'm never timid but this subject makes me nervous.

His eyes widen. "Has that happened to you?"

I nod my head. "Yes, it started a few days before we left town. It started as just a dream I thought, but it turned out I wasn't dreaming. I started waking up with my things floating over my bed."

Father sucks in air and takes a big gulp before continuing "Well, that definitely counts as powers. It appears you really will have magical abilities." His voice comes out almost awed and he pulls me into a big bear hug before holding me an arm's length away.

"No worries, pumpkin, we will get through this." He ruffles my hair exactly like he used to do when I was a kid worried about something minor.

As a kid, those worries were trivial but now, this isn't

trivial. I might have magical powers? How is this real life? What is happening to me?

He didn't really answer my questions, but I decide I'll ask him more about it later. Right now all I want to do is get into some warm, dry clothes. The only positive thing about finding out I have magical powers is now I know the reason my things started soaring around my room of their own accord.

10

ATTINA

THE NEXT MORNING, AFTER I COLLECT WOOD FOR THE DAY AND Father and I eat breakfast, I follow him back to that fallen log and cross the creek, back to the spot where he was practicing yesterday.

Today, Father is carrying two swords, one sheathed on his side and one across his back. When we make it across the creek he unsheathes the sword on his back, arcing it over his head in one swift motion, and hands the sword over to me.

"Today we're going to learn swordplay."

In my hands, the sword feels awkward, like some foreign object that doesn't belong there. Both my hands grip the handle and I hold the sword out a respectful distance with the tip pointed to the ground.

"Attina, what are you doing?" Father admonishes.

I study the sword as I answer. "I'm afraid I'm going to hurt myself and accidentally cut off a finger or something.

"Well the only way you're going to get over that fear is by practicing with it."

I give him a look, I exaggeratedly widen my eyes and

shrug my shoulders, which I hope shows him I think he's crazy. He ignores my scowl and walks past me up to a huge old knotty Pine tree.

"I want you to swing and hit this tree. Once on the right side then again on the left; over and over until I say stop.

"Ugh that's ridiculous. I can't chop that thing down." I complain, more nervous than upset.

"I don't want you to chop it down. You need to get used to the weight and feel of a real sword."

"Yes, I understand Father." I hesitantly lift the heavy sword and swing it, slashing it into the Pine's bark. I feel the repercussion of the strike vibrate up my arms and down my back. I do the same on the other side and feel that same sensation again.

Without taking my eyes off the tree I say, "I don't know if I can do this."

"You can do this Attina. I know you can." He puts his hand on my elbow and lifts it into a different position. "Choke up on the hilt." I glare at him, confused at the terminology and he chuckles. "The handle, choke up on the handle."

I do as he says and feel a lightness in the sword I didn't feel a second before.

"Lift your elbow a little bit more. I want you to swing this the same way you swung the ax this morning. Can you do that?" I nod as he continues, "Just instead of swinging the ax downward, you're swinging it sideways."

I nod my head again. "The vibrations after making contact with the tree; I don't know if I can handle those."

Father steps in front of me and looks me right in the eyes. "Yes, you can. When you use this sword on a person and you hit bone it will make the same vibration. It's something you need to get used to."

"But isn't there some other way we can do this?"

I feel like all this swinging is going to hurt and I'm already in agonizing pain from our other training yesterday, so a day wielding this sword does not sound appealing.

He doesn't answer right away, simply stares at me for a second, then turns and walks away shouting over his shoulder "You know what. I don't need to explain myself to you; get it done. I'll be back later. Keep practicing until then. Get to it." Almost as an afterthought he adds, "And I'll know if you put in the work or not, so just do it."

I roll my eyes but do as he says. I strike the tree over and over. Soon my arms, shoulders, and back begin aching and it gets worse and worse as the day progresses. By the time Father stops me for lunch I can barely lift the sword.

Father glances at my shaking arms and the tree, which now has huge chunks missing from it. "Looks like you worked hard today, I'm proud of you. Now let's get some grub." He takes the sword from my hands and we head back to camp for lunch.

After lunch he brings me back to the other side of the creek again. I walk up to the same old pine tree and turn around, hand out, waiting for Father to hand me the sword once more but this time he puts a long thick branch in my hand instead. When did he pick that up? How did I miss him picking it up?

"What's this for?" I ask.

"We're going to train you for a real fight. You don't want to learn how to sword fight with actual swords right off do you?"

I instantly have a flash of my hand being chopped off and vigorously shake my head. Father winks at me and lifts a stick, almost identical to the one in my hand. Father swings his stick at my head without warning but at the last possible moment I lift my stick, blocking the blow. I feel the vibration from the hit all the way into my toes. He's obviously not holding back even with just a stick. I'm so glad these aren't real swords.

We parry back and forth the rest of the day. Father has hit me with his stick over and over. Anytime I let down my guard, even for one second. He's right there smacking my arm, stomach, or back. The pain when he hits me is acute and fierce and by the time we finish, I feel like one big bruise. But even through the pain, I can tell I've made some progress today. Father steps up to me and takes my "sword" from me and leans it against the Oak tree I was attacking this morning.

"You did good today. You take after your mother so much. She was a quick learner too." Hearing about our similarities makes me beam with pride.

As Father turns and walks away, I ask, "Are you ready for dinner then? Are we done for the day?" I cross my fingers hoping we're done; I'm starving.

"We have one more thing I want to get done today before we start dinner." Of course my stomach picks that exact time to growl. Both our eyes drift down at my stomach and laugh. Father then walks away past our little bridge, not crossing over it. I continue after him.

"It's very important you know how to navigate new territory, even in the dark. In battle you usually only have a passing glance at your surroundings to figure out where you are. Taking a wrong turn in battle could be the difference between life and death. To teach you this, we're going to walk through the forest for a while to kind of orient you then we'll head back to camp and have dinner. After dinner I'll blindfold you and bring you back into the forest and leave you somewhere. Then you'll have to find your way back to camp on your own."

This surprises me. "Okay," I reply. Father simply glances over his shoulder and smiles at me.

After dinner we head out. Father leaves the blindfold off until we cross the creek, then the blindfold is on and he holds my hand as he guides me deeper into the forest.

I hear Father's voice. "Even though we walked around this area only a couple hours ago, everything you see will seem different when I pull off the blindfold. You haven't been out on your own at night; things seem and sound different in the dark. You might get scared, but you can do this Attina. You are scarier than anything out here. Remember that."

It takes awhile, but Father eventually stops us. He turns me around and I think he'll take off my blindfold but he keeps turning me around and around until I'm not sure which way we came from anymore. When I'm good and well confused he releases me.

I reach up to pull off the blindfold. "Don't take it off just yet, pumpkin. Count to one-hundred so I have time to leave and then you can pull it off and head back to camp. See you back at camp, pumpkin!" he shouts. I can tell he's already walking away from how distant his voice sounds.

I count to one hundred and pull off the blindfold. *This shouldn't be too hard. Yeah I haven't ever been out after dark, but it can't be so different from being out during the day.*

It doesn't take me being out in the dark very long for me to figure out just how wrong I was.

In the dark everything, exactly like Father said, looks completely different. Within the first few minutes I'm jumping at every little leaf moving in the breeze. All I can think of is there must be something in the dark ready to attack me, but I don't hear anything except the wind blowing softly.

After I get my racing thoughts under control, I walk in the direction I last heard Father's voice but it doesn't take long for me to realize I'm heading the wrong way.

By now I should at least be hearing water running from the creek. I know all I have to do is find the water and follow it back to camp. Then through my thoughts I hear a soft coo which almost sounds conspiratorial. I think it must be an owl. I haven't ever seen one in real life so I peer up, but I don't see an owl; I see a red-tailed hawk.

One big ass hawk.

It's so much bigger than a normal hawk, and as my eyes scan over it I see its eyes glowing in the darkness. Not the normal glow of predators at night but like two candles; and they are staring directly at me. I feel myself stop breathing, all the air leaves my lungs and a shiver pulses along my skin.

All the bird does is stare at me; it's scrutiny planting me to the ground. I've had plenty of animals gawk at me throughout my years of hunting but this is the first time an animal has made me feel like this. I'm so frightened I feel cold, frozen to the spot, as if a bucket of cold water was thrown over my head. I swear it's sizing me up, but such a thing isn't possible; it's an animal, animals don't have such cognitive power. I'm not sure how long we stand there staring each other down, but I don't move until the bird moves.

I instantly feel like a prey animal that just now spotted a predator, ready to pounce. The hawk swoops down at me, it's huge wings barely fitting between the tree trunks. His sharp dagger sized talons are extended, ready to grab on to me, and he's aiming for my face. As soon as the hawk takes flight I pitch myself sideways.

I throw my arm up blocking my face and dive next to a tree—shocked because I don't know how I could have moved so fast—as I feel a warmth stroke my muscles. The coarse bark of the tree I dove into grabs onto my shoulder and scratches my skin. The hawk almost hits the ground before lifting off again and flying high into the night sky, disappearing behind the trees.

I take a moment and rest there on the forest floor trying to wrap my mind around what just happened. Was that a normal hawk? No way. If it wasn't a normal hawk, then what was it, and what was it doing out here in this forest? I'll have to remember to talk to Father about this, but for now I need to figure a way to get back to camp.

By now I should have run into the creek, at the very least I should be able to hear it. I browse around me and take a deep steadying breath. I need to keep my wits about me. Only one solution comes to mind, I need to walk in widening concentric circles until I can hear the water and then walk toward the sound and follow the creek back to camp.

I walk and walk but all I hear is the rustling of leaves and trees swaying in the wind. I feel my chest tighten. What if I'm lost? How would Father find me? If I'm truly lost, I doubt even he could find me. I don't even have a weapon with me so I couldn't hunt for food or protect myself from predators.

Then, right when I'm about to give into these thoughts and completely breakdown crying, I hear running water. It took me ten long circles to find it, but I did it.

I walk toward the sound and it leads me to the creek. I follow it up and after what feels like forever I see our camp-fire. It's almost daybreak now. Father must have kept it lit all night long.

As I stride out of the tree line, I can see the beautiful pink and orange of the morning skyline. On the other side of camp the horses both sleep, sprawled out on their sides. I crawl into my tent and leave the questions I have for my father for tomorrow.

I wake to the sound of my tent rattling, as I am rubbing the sleep out of my eyes Raven pokes her baby doll head in. When she sees me laying down she instantly rolls her beautiful gray eyes and says, "What are you doing, it's daylight."

I sit up, oh no, I'm late. Great, I'm late, and Raven out of everyone got sent to get me up. Raven shakes her head. "Your father has something planned for you since you decided you wanted to sleep in. Your mother never would have done something so childish."

I throw my clothes on and meekly crawl out of my tent. Father is sitting by the fire sipping on his morning cup of coffee after a long draw on his coffee he glares at me and says in his harsh incensed "you're in trouble voice". "This is the last of the wood, I suggest you hurry up and cut the rest of the wood we will need for the day, then get back here and we'll start your lessons." I groan and turn to start my morning trek, then from behind I hear Father whisper, "Today will be fun." And it's then and there I know today will not be fun.

I finish my task and bring the wood back to camp. When I finish cutting and stacking it, I head over to the fire to grab some of the breakfast Father made while I was gone. He made my favorite, bacon and eggs with biscuits and gravy. I am about to take my first bite of biscuits when I hear

Father's gravelly voice behind me. "What do you think you're doing?"

I turn to glance up at him and say, "I'm eating." He snatches the plate out of my hands and throws the plate and all into the fire pit. "You haven't earned food yet, your little stunt this morning made sure of that."

"But Father, I didn't do it on purpose." I can feel the tears welling up. Anyone who knows me knows the one way to break me is to deny me food.

"Attina, I don't care if you meant to do it or not. It happened. If you're going to do this, get your kingdom back and save your people, even something this innocent and benign is a big deal. You need to be a well oiled machine, which won't happen with you sleeping in, no matter how late your night was the night before. Now get up, you need to learn a lesson about discipline, we're going for a run."

As we run, I try to talk to Father about the hawk last night, but he shrugs me off, reminding me things seems different at night. I know he's angry about this morning but him assuming I was being hysterical last night hurts my feelings.

We run through the forest for miles and miles. I don't know how long we've run but by the time we make it back to camp my legs feel like two mushy stumps and knives slice through my lungs. I can feel every bit of oxygen filling my lungs, but no matter how hard I breathe I can't catch my breath.

When we finally make it back to camp Father announces while he walks off to pet Raven, "Okay Attina, take a break and then we'll get back to the real training." Oak strides to where I've collapsed by the back of my tent and nuzzles my chest. I grab onto his head and give him a big bear hug, my words failing me.

As usual though, Oak knows exactly what I need to hear. "You're doing great, Attina. Don't listen to Raven, I know she can be vicious, but she truly can be loving. You will get through this, I promise you. I can see it in you. You have such a strong will and big heart, if anyone can defeat Henrik it's you."

"Henrik? How do you know about Henrik?" I wheeze.

"I was with your mother when she was his top slayer. Raven was just a baby when we left the castle with your mother, so she doesn't remember much but I still do."

My jaw drops "What?" I hadn't connected the fact that Oak must have been my mother's mount. He's a Fae horse. She was Fae. It should have hit me sooner, but this is the first time I've realized Oak must know so much about my mother. I have so many questions for him.

But that's the exact moment Father decides to call to me. "Okay Attina, time to get back to work"

I start to get up gingerly, Oak puts his head down to help me get on my feet. I wrap my arms around his massive head and pull. As I get up I give him a few pets on his neck and say, "We have a lot to talk about tonight after training. You've been holding out on me, Oak". I give Oak a wink and start off towards my father.

While I'd been resting with Oak, Father walked over to the creek and is now standing by his fallen tree. As I reach him, he crosses the creek and I slowly follow. My body is so weak, I wobble back and forth on the tree trunk, trying to keep my balance. More than once I almost fall into the creek. Father leaves me and walks over to where he was training yesterday while I flounder trying to cross the creek.

As I catch up Father turns to me. "Okay, now I want to see your bow skills". From behind a tree he pulls out a stunningly beautiful bow. He smiles and winks at me as he hands me the bow.

In my hands, the bow feels smooth and warm. The riser fits so perfectly in my hand that it could have been carved specifically for me. The upper and lower limbs are made out of a black locust wood and the string is made out of something so black it seems to pull in all the colors around it. It reminds me of Oak's mane and tail.

I peek over at Father and ask, "What is this string made out of? It feels familiar."

He chuckles "I made that out of Oak's tail it's 20 strands of Fae horse tail, the strongest material you can find on the planet, you won't ever have to restring it."

The upper and lower limbs are carved to depict the goddess of hunting with her dogs and horses chasing some sort of deer I'd never seen with three sets of horns. I glance from the carvings up to my father.

"Your mother helped me carve it. It's the goddess of hunting. She's hunting an animal, which represents all the things she protects—animals, childbirth, virginity, hunting, archery, and the moon. Each horn represents one of those categories."

He takes in a deep steadying breath. Talking about this memory is obviously hard for him, but then he continues, "I know you're handy with a bow but I'd like to see how good you really are."

Father hands me three arrows out of his full quiver. I grasp the arrows he hands me. They seem like normal arrows but there is something different about them. I can feel it—Same metal, same arrowheads, same smooth pinewood, but the fletching...something is different about the fletching.

I can tell as soon as I run my fingers over the stiff, hazel feathers these aren't normal bird feathers. These feathers glisten in the sunlight refracting a rainbow of colors, and I can feel a warmth coming from them, which I've felt some-where else before, but they also hold an evilness.

I glance up to Father. "What animal are these feathers from?"

Father tilts his head down at me, a quizzical expression on his face. "Just curious, how did you know they were different?"

"I just felt it, okay? So what's the deal?"

"What did you feel?"

"Ugh okay, they feel warm. I've felt it before but I'm not sure where."

He holds his chin and nods his head "Interesting."

Father turns to me and points to the arrow. "Those are from a Fae hawk your grandfather's Fae hawk to be exact, his number one spy. While your mother was with the Fae, she only used arrows with Fae hawk fletching. She told me those feathers make the arrows fly faster and truer than normal arrows."

"But for today's exercise let's use these normal arrows." As he says this, he pulls three different arrows out of his quiver. I can tell the difference right away, there is no energy coming off of these arrows and the feathers on the fletching is a dull brown.

"Why did you hand me these arrows then?" I ask while switching arrows with him.

"I was curious if you could tell by touch that they were different from regular arrows or not." He winks at me.

"Okay, now show me what you've got, pumpkin." Step-ping back, he points down range at a target. I hadn't even noticed the target until now. Up in a tree on the range I see a stump dangling from one of its branches by a long rope.

The stump has two concentric circles smudged in black ash, which is obviously ash from one of our nightly fires.

I knock an arrow and smile.

Today I'd felt like nothing but a failure from the moment I woke up, now I have a chance to actually show what I can do. I can finally redeem myself. I pull the end of the arrow and the string to the corner of my lips like I've done thousands of times before, like James taught me all those years ago.

I take in a deep breath and let it out slowly. I wait and in between breaths when I am steadiest I line up my arrow with the center of the target and gently release the arrow. I blink for a split second and when I open my eyes again the arrow is stuck dead in the center of the target.

I'd taken my time with my first shot mostly for show. I turn and glance at Father with a smirk on my face. In one swift movement, I turn, draw, and loose a second arrow, this one cutting through the rope holding the stump to the tree. The stump falls to the ground with a cracking thud.

In quick succession I fire the last arrow. As I move, I can feel the energy build up from my arms and through my chest causing the bow to feel like it is humming in my hand. Without watching where the arrow lands I turn to Father, a big shit-eating grin plastered on my face. "Well, was that good enough?"

Father's jaw clenches and he has a strange sheen to his face, almost a green sickly coloring. I spin around as fast as my body will allow me to but don't see anyone or anything around us which would elicit such a shocking response from him. I turn back to Father but he seems to have gotten his composure.

"Is that normal for you?" he says, pointing at the target behind me.

I spin around again and this time I see it.

My last arrow was aimed to cut the rope tied on the tree branch in half making the rope fall to the ground, but the arrow hadn't only stopped there. It had continued on through the thick branch until it snapped. Now, instead of the sturdy branch which was there seconds ago, the branch is hanging on by one last string of bark.

I stand there in awe with my jaw hanging open. I don't know how long I stay like that before Father places his hand on my shoulder.

"Your Awakening is about to start. Fae are stronger and faster than humans, you'll notice things like this happening more often now," he says ominously as he walks back to camp. I stand there in shock for a moment.

"Awakening?" What's my Awakening? Wait isn't that when I get magical powers? I'm so confused, but I decide not to worry about it at the moment and follow Father back to camp.

As we walk back to the river crossing, Father calls over his shoulder, "That bow is yours now, Attina." I am shocked. This is the only thing I know of that he and Mother made together, besides me.

"No, Father. I can't take this from you."

Father turns back to me smiling, placing his hand on my shoulder. "Yes you can. You can use that bow to its full potential like I never could. I am so happy to give you something like this," he says nodding to the bow. "And I know your mother would be happy too, pumpkin". He kisses my forehead, and I don't know what to say to him so we finish making our way back to camp in silence.

As we get back to camp Father doesn't walk to our tents like I think he will but stops right inside the sparring ring. I stop outside the ring and call out to him, "Wait, I thought we were done for the day".

Father belly laughs. "What made you think that? You lost or broke all three arrows back there just to show off. We're gonna work off some of your arrogance."

I think he'll have us go for another run, but no, we get back to sparring instead. This time it's full force and I continue to have to pick myself up off the ground. I know I'll have a myriad bruises tomorrow. I feel like I won't ever get good at this.

"Stop hitting me so hard!" I yell at him as I throw my full weight behind a punch, which misses him completely, catapulting me off balance.

"You have to know what it feels like to be hit by someone bigger than yourself. You can't know what it feels like until you've been through it. Now get up and try again."

The rest of the day is spent sparring. Father shows me some more technical things he's learned. How to hold my hand, so I don't break my fingers when I hit someone, to use my weight, to throw that weight behind my punch without falling, how to stand with my shoulders and legs so I'll be stable, even how to use my opponent's weight against them.

By the end of our session, I can barely make it to my tent. I feel like my whole body is one big bruise and I'm in more pain than I thought possible and exhausted, so as soon as my head hits my sleeping bag on top of the hard ground, I pass out.

11

———

ATTINA

Before I know it the sun is peeking over the treetops and my father is throwing open my tent.

"Wake up, pumpkin. I know you're exhausted from the past few days, but it's time to gather and cut wood for the day. This is the one and only day I will wake you up. Don't get used to this, but after yesterday's workout and the night before, you deserve it," he says smiling.

I don't know what has him in such a good this morning, but I will never be a morning person, so I groan while I start moving to dress. As he leaves to give me privacy, Father calls back, "Wake me when it's done," and I can hear him crawling back into his tent. As soon as I finish splitting wood for the day, I call to Father so we can start another day of training.

Today is another day full of sparring and pain. My fingers start aching and I know my father can tell I'm pulling my punches. Then, he puts his hands down, stepping toward me.

"You're just going to keep hurting yourself and you won't

get any better if you continue punching like this," he says as he grabs hold of my hands.

I wince at the contact and Father sees me recoil.

"Your hands wouldn't be hurting if you were punching the way I showed you." He grabs my wobbling little finger and I rip my hands out of his.

"Ow! Why would you do that?" I shout, cradling my hand as best as I can.

"You can't land your punches on your pinkie. There is little to no power there and you're going to end up breaking your fingers punching like that." He lifts up his own hand and points to the space between his middle and forefinger. "You need to start landing your punches here if you want to seriously hurt someone."

"Fine," I say with an edge in my voice.

Father chuckles, "Good, use that anger."

I immediately cool my temper. "I'm not mad at you. I'm mad at myself."

"I know, pumpkin you've always been like that. As I said use your anger; take it out on me, I can take it."

I nod my head and start throwing punches into his palms again. After the first few punches, I can feel a difference. My pinkie still hurts, but now I can feel more power coming from my punches, and as I relax I can see my little finger is no longer wobbling.

"Good," Father says. "Let's get you some lunch and we can try again afterwards."

While Father is cooking us lunch, I head over to visit with the horses. Oak and Raven are both lying down, sunbathing by our camp. When I approach, Oak sits up on his front end to gap at me, but as soon as Raven sees me she flips her entire body over so her back is facing me.

"So, how did today go?" Oak asks with hope in his voice. I just groan at him and roll my eyes.

"That bad huh?" Oak whispers.

Immediately Raven lifts her head and snorts. "Of course she failed, it was inevitable. She will never be her mother."

This hurts me. I don't know how many times over the years Raven has said those exact words, but now, since I'm learning more about my mother and myself, the words hit me like a sting. Usually, I simply ignore her snarky comments, but this time I can't.

I glare over at Raven's back and ask, "Why are you always so mean to me?"

Raven picks her head up slightly. "Humph. I'm not even going to dignify such a ridiculous question with an answer." Then turns her head back away from me.

I glance back to Oak, tears filling my eyes and say, "Sorry, I just can't," and stand up and walk back to the tents to eat lunch.

After lunch is over it's back to the sparring ring. What Raven said to me before lunch has me feeling incensed. I start throwing punches as I keep replaying our conversation over and over in my mind. Of course I failed? Like I didn't ever have a chance. Who is she to belittle me? I'm getting better. How can she judge me so harshly?

I feel myself vibrating with the anger swelling inside of me. The vibration turns into a heat. The heat starts from my hurt heart and leeches out into my arms then into my hands. I punch harder and faster trying to release all that heat, to get it out of me before it consumes me. Then from the haze of anger, I can hear my father call to me.

"Attina! Baby! Stop!"

His frantic voice pulls me out of the world I was lost in a

second ago and I take a step back. Father's eyes are wide, but his hands are still up ready for me, willing to take the burning hit if I need it. I see the smoke drifting off his outstretched hands. Then I stare down to my own hands and they are pulsing red, like I have fire in my veins thrumming through me.

I drop my hands and run over to my father flinging my arms around his neck. "I'm so sorry! Are you okay? Whaa... what happened?" As I pull away from him I see his eyes have softened.

"Yes, pumpkin. I'm fine, just surprised is all. I guess we'll just have to wrap our hands during sparring from now on." He runs a hand through his short peppered hair and chuckles. I glance back down to my own hands and see they've gone back to my normal skin color.

"Don't worry. You're coming into your Awakening, that's it. So, what got you so angry?"

I can feel my anger clouding my judgment so much I don't even think to ask what he means about my Awakening. "Raven. She thinks I'm useless and won't ever be anything like my mother."

"And what about her words angered you so bad?" he asks, crossing his arms and glaring at me like he's annoyed.

Meekly I say, "Well, who is she to judge me?" Suddenly I feel embarrassed so I wrap my arms around myself.

"Exactly, Attina, who is she?"

"What? I don't understand."

"Why do you care what she thinks? If you're going to succeed, you can't let people get to you like that."

"Yeah but—"

He cuts me off. "No buts. Everyone will be challenging you, underestimating you and trying to bring you down. If you lose your head like this every time something like this happens you'll never beat Henrik and take your throne. You have to be harder and slicker than that, Attina."

He takes a deep breath and lets it out. "Now, we're going to try another tactic and work all your anger out of you." He steps up in front of me and puts his leg behind me like he's about to walk around me and pushes the front of my shoulders hard making me fall over his leg to the ground.

I hit the ground hard flat on my back, which knocks all the air straight out of my lungs. I gasp for air and from the ground I yell, "What did you do that for?"

"You need to learn some grappling skills and this will take some of that anger out of you."

He goes over the basics with me, showing me how to use someone's weight or height against them, the best places to strike, how to get out of holds, and even which bones are the easiest to break. After the basics we even start mixing in these techniques with our sparring... the results are not promising.

I push myself up off the ground where my father has once again knocked me. This is going nowhere, I am just getting thrown to the ground and collecting more bruises.

"Father, this is useless, I'm not getting any better."

My father glances at me for a second then smiles. "Yes, I agree this isn't working. Take a ten minute break, and let's try something different."

For my break, I decide I better have the talk with Oak, which I've been meaning to have with him.

"Hey old man, you have a minute to talk?" I ask as I walk up to him out in the field by camp.

Oak bows to me. "For you anything my lady."

"You knew my mother and didn't tell me. Now I want to hear it all. Tell me everything you know," I say with more authority and accusation in my voice than I mean for.

"What do you want to know my lady?" he asks honestly.

"Like I said Oak, everything."

"Hmm... Okay, well I guess it's best to start from the beginning. I was extremely young when your mother was born. The only thing I really remember from that time was how happy everyone was. She was the new heir and would one day be queen. The slaves who took care of Fae animals spoke freely in front of a young horse like me. They had hopes the king would be different, maybe kinder, after his first child was born, and if that didn't happen maybe she would be a more gentle leader."

"Which she never got the chance to be," I whisper.

Oak drops his head to the ground and shakes his head. "No, she did not, but her legacy does not die with her. You will be the kind, gentle Queen which she didn't have the chance to be."

I sniff back tears. "Yes, you're right." I nod. "Now get back to the story, mister." I point an accusatory finger at him.

Oak chuckles. "Yes, back to the story. Umm where was I?"

"The human slaves hoped she would be a more gentle leader," I reply.

"Yes. Well as soon as your mother was old enough to walk she was constantly at the palace stables. You could always find her there." Oak chuckles. "I guess you could say your mother and I grew up together. She took a liking to me since we were both around the same age. We went on so many adventures in the forest growing up. As a kid she was almost as wild and unruly as you were." He winks at me.

"Before long, she knew Shadow Forest better than prob-ably anyone on all of Arealea. She even had a hideout deep in the forest. I don't really remember when we found it exactly but buried deep in the forest she found an ancient tree bigger than all the rest of the trees in the forest. I think that tree chose to show itself to her because she searched, and there is no mention of such a tree in any of the ancient texts in the Fae palace. It was obviously a magical tree. She would walk up to it and place her hands on its hulking bark and a door only big enough for her would open up. I don't know what she did in there, but I know it was her sanctum as a child and continued to be so well into adulthood. She even got the necklace you're wearing out of that tree. How she convinced it to give her jewelry is beyond me." Oak chuckles and I grab at my necklace. It's comforting knowing this necklace came from somewhere which brought my mother such happiness.

"Anyway," Oak continues, "I've strayed from the story again. I was there with her through every fall, every cut, and every fight. When she wanted to join the army, she confided in me. I was her friend, her confidant, and her partner in crime. I don't think I could have ever gotten over her death if it wasn't for you my lady. You gave me a purpose again."

I launch myself on Oak wrapping my arms around his neck. "I love you so much. You've always been my partner in crime too. I'm so glad I have you in my life. I don't know what I would ever do without you, Oak."

Oak puts his head over my shoulder and takes a step towards me so his head and neck wraps around me, hugging me back as he says, "I do not ever intend on leaving your side my lady."

I later find out Father's idea of "something different" is to head out for a run around the forest for an hour. After our run, I crawl back into camp and he and I sit across the campfire from each other eating our dinner. Father's eyes are fixated on the fire, like he's searching for answers in the way the fire crackles and flicks.

"I've been pushing off this talk, Attina, and I'm sorry, I guess I was trying to spare you from such a big load on your shoulders all at once."

"Father we had this conversation before, you told me all about my mother and who I really am," I say annoyed, how could he already forget.

"No, pumpkin. I need to tell you what's been going on since we left town."

"Oh, I've been meaning to ask you when you're planning for us to set off back to town so we can leave for Sanctuary with everyone."

"We're not, pumpkin. We're staying here."

Panic grips me. "Did something happen? What's going on? Is everyone okay?"

"Attina, everyone is fine... to my knowledge. It's nothing like you're thinking," he says, shaking his head for emphasis.

This does little to soothe me and with panic clearly coating my voice I ask, "Well then what is it? Stop keeping things from me! I deserve to know everything. Stop keeping me in the dark like I'm a child!!!"

"Yes, I know you're right, you're not a child anymore but you will forever be my baby girl, and I will forever try to protect you from unpleasant things if I can. First off, the town is no more..." I feel myself begin hyperventilating, but Father presses on. "The townspeople left. They're traveling to Sanctuary, the hidden town covered in rock we talked about in the last town meeting."

I let out a huge sigh, relieved to know everyone is okay. I can feel the air slowly coming back into my lungs as I continue.

"When did this happen? How do you know this? I thought we had almost a week before everyone left. I thought you had packed too much for a week trip, but I trusted you would get us back before the move. Those are *our* people. How could you let them leave without us?"

"Yes, pumpkin those are our people, but after the town meeting when we got home, you went off to bed, James left, and I took off to go to Nathan's house to talk with him. Nathan is the only other person in the world that knows who your mother truly was. We talked until dawn and came up with a plan." He paused before continuing.

"As you know, the Solis have gotten out of control and too close to home. We decided he would take as many people from the town to Sanctuary as he could get to leave right away and I would take you out to this campsite and explain things to you and train you. After we're done training and you've gone through your Awakening we can set out for Sanctuary."

"I still don't understand why we couldn't have stayed with them, gone to Sanctuary, and trained there."

Father takes a deep, steadying breath and gazes back into the fire, his face goes stern. "Which brings me to the other thing I needed to tell you about, pumpkin. You will be going through a change soon."

I roll my eyes. "Father, I already went through puberty years ago."

"Attina," he says in a no nonsense voice. "Not like that. When Fae turn a certain age, they go through a change; their Awakening, and when this happens magic is what's awakened."

"Each Fae is different. Some can control one or multiple elements, some can speak to spirits, and even fewer can listen in on people's thoughts. A Fae's powers could be literally anything under the sun according to your mother. Your mother's power was weather manipulation."

"She said when a Fae comes of age there is a power which is released, a power so forceful it makes the ground quake. She said that's what earthquakes actually are: a Fae coming into their power. This power is the magic awakening inside them, but along with this massive power, bursts pain. Your mother said when she came of age it felt like the power would break her in two. Now, I know you've grown up with these townspeople your whole life, but they've all grown up hating the Fae. Do you seriously think you'd be able to hide your Fae side when the magic inside you is awakened?"

That startles me; I can feel the tears welling up inside me. It hadn't actually hit me yet but now it does—I am a freak of nature. There is no one like me in the entire world we know of. I belong with no one.

The tears start rolling down my face with a vengeance. Father stands up from his place across the campfire and sits by my side, worry is written all across his features, his brow is furrowed and his lips sag, like this is not the reaction he was expecting. Tears are pouring from my eyes now mixing with liquid coming out of my nose. I wipe the cold wetness from my face and all my emotions overcome me as soon as my Father puts his hand on my shoulder reassuringly. I can't help myself. I snatch at my mother's necklace, rubbing it desperately, trying to soothe myself.

I start screaming. "Why would you do this to me?"

Father pulls his hand away from me with shock written across his features. "What do you mean, Attina?"

"I belong nowhere, I can't show my true self to humans or Fae. Why would you and Mother create such a freak?" I shout and stand up before running to my tent. When I get inside, I flip onto my sleeping bag and let the tears flow freely.

I hear Father walk up outside my tent.

He clears his throat and quietly says "Pumpkin, we both love you for you. You are perfect exactly the way you are. As far as your mother and I are concerned, you're the best of both worlds. Others will see it too."

I stay quiet. I can't face him right now with my emotions running wild inside me. I hear him blow out a breath and walk away to silently crawl into his tent. I cry my heart out, falling asleep while my tears dry on my cheeks.

12

ATTINA

I WAKE UP THE NEXT MORNING WITH THE RISING SUN AND HEAD off to chop wood for the day. While I'm splitting wood, Father walks up to me. I'm about to apologize for my behavior last night when he interrupts me.

"We're running out of meat, I need you to go on a hunt for us."

"Okay!" I say enthusiastically. I can use the break from training to do something I'm good at. Hunting is something I know how to do and am comfortable doing. With a jump in my step, I walk over to Oak and lead him back to where our packs and saddles are.

"You ready for another hunting trip bud?" I say as I pet his soft velvety muzzle.

"Forever, my lady," Oak says, bowing his head. I throw my saddle up on his back and I'm starting to cinch him up when I hear my Father behind me.

"No, pumpkin. Today I want you to use Raven." He smiles sweetly.

My father knows Raven and I don't get along and he's asking this? Is this punishment for last night?

"Ugh, Father, I will hunt better with Oak. We've been hunting off and on together for years, we know how to work together," I plead.

"I know, but I want you and Raven to bond ,which will only happen if you two are forced to be together alone. You both need to learn to rely on each other."

I roll my eyes making sure Father sees my annoyance.

"Fine," I say with too much force and attitude in my voice. Then I call out to my arch-enemy, who is off on the other side of camp eating.

"Raven, get over here, we're going hunting." Raven does not even lift her head to acknowledge me so I call again. "Come on Raven, we need to get going". Again there is no hint of acknowledgement I exist or said anything.

I turn to Father, frustrated he is putting me through this. He knows she doesn't like me, and I sure don't have any love for her, and yet he is still putting us through this.

By this time, Father is sitting by the low fire sipping his morning coffee slowly. He barely moves his head and sends out a loud whistle. Before I know it, Raven has trotted over to Father's side with a triumphant shit-eating grin plastered across her muzzle. Father gives her a pet on the shoulder and I walk over to them with a halter and grab her from him. For all the nonsense she started, I tie her up to a tree while I saddle her to ensure no more funny business.

After I finish saddling, I pull her away from the tree and put my leg up into the stirrup. As I swing my other leg over Raven's back she spins underneath me. I almost soar off the backend of her, but at the last moment I am able to hook my foot around the back of the saddle and pull myself back up on top of her.

"Knock it off, Raven!" I admonish. From behind us, I hear my Father chuckling under his breath.

I yell out, "Yeah, thank you so much for all the help over there, Mister Chuckles," as I throw a seething glance over my shoulder. I take a glimpse behind me to see Oak standing next to Father. Oak's eyes are wide and his mouth hangs wide open, he's obviously shocked at what just happened.

Raven and I walk through the forest for a few hours before I search for a perfect spot to stop and lay in wait for our prey. I want to get far away from the scent of camp, and with my years of hunting experience I know a prey animal will stay far away from the smells and noises coming from camp.

We walk parallel to the creek until it opens up to another pasture. There are trails to and from the creek leading back to a mass of trees. It's a spot where the water slows enough it becomes a perfect spot for animals to drink. I climb down off Raven and walk to her face.

"I need you to hide out of sight, you might spook the prey. Keep within earshot though, in case I need you." I put my hands on either side of her baby doll head, making sure she's staring directly into my eyes "Please, please, please don't leave me, and please listen for me. I know there is no love lost between us, but Father is counting on us to get this food." I can hear the pleading in my voice and it's so embarrassing.

Raven's eyes flick away and then look me directly in the eye again. "You think I don't know that? I wish he would have let you take Oak, but I will do my duty and take care of you until we get this food back to him". Then she snorts and turns around trotting off. Over her shoulder she shouts, "Don't screw this up kid!"

I think this is the first time she's called me something

other than a failure. Maybe I'm growing on her? Who knows, miracles do happen.

I watch her walk away and my attention is grabbed by a glimpse of something on the ridge she's walking towards. Is that a person up there? It's only a shadow though, like air is flowing through the form. I rub my eyes thinking that maybe I'm seeing things, and when I glance back nothing is there. My mind must be playing tricks on me.

I climb up a huge pine tree that is situated between the creek and the tree line. It's obvious animals travel closely to this tree often by the way the grass is pushed down around it. I climb into the tree and onto a thick branch to wait with my new bow, an ordinary arrow pulled out at the ready, caressing the pictures my parents carved into it all those years ago. I have my eyes peeled on the tree line the rest of the day, but nothing appears.

Then, right as the sun starts to set I see it. A young lone deer creeps out of the tree line far to the left of where I'm sitting, too far out for me to get a clear shot with my bow. Part of being a good hunter is to know your limitations. Such a shot would be too far for me to kill the deer cleanly. So, I wait.

I wait for the deer to get a few hundred yards closer. He's awfully slow and cautious so I can't make any noise at all or I'm sure to spook him away. I slowly pull back the string of my bow and stay in that position, following his movement.

Then I hear a howl— a howl so loud and deep it shakes the ground. There's no way that's only one wolf, it's too loud, but it doesn't sound like multiple wolves either, just one voice, one deep deafening roar.

The deer stops its movement completely frozen in time. A few seconds later another howl is let out again, but this time much closer. The deer seems suspended in time but then it takes off like a shot, in a race for its life and is lost across the creek and through the woods on the other side. I'm so shocked from the deafening howl I don't even lose an arrow as the deer races past me.

No reason for me to stay here any longer, especially with a wolf in the area spooking off all the game animals.

I whistle for Raven and strap the bow and arrow back on my back. I seriously hope she didn't ditch me. With how our relationship has been over the years, it wouldn't surprise me if she left me here to prove again that I'm nothing like my mother. I don't hear Raven coming and I spin to focus back on the tree line where the howl came from and the tree line is moving, almost swaying. I whistle again, this time it's a more high-pitched, urgent whistle.

That's when I hear a whinny and see Raven running as fast as her legs will take her to the tree I'm crouching in. She runs to the base of the tree and right as she gets there the ground shakes with another deep menacing howl.

The ground shakes so violently I have to hold onto the trunk of the tree to keep from falling out. I can hear the trees strain and crack, then the trees to the right of us bend and break open to make room for a huge wolf. It looks like a whole pack of wolves smashed into one creature.

The wolf's fur is almost as shocking as its size. The fur isn't any one particular color but seems to pulsate from brown to gray to black, like it's fur is constantly changing with the foliage around it. The wolf is snarling and drooling while it scans the landscape. Its searching eyes focus on me and I see its mouth move into almost a smile, which is impossible, wolves don't smile.

I feel immobilized by fear. I grab on to the tree trunk

hard, the wolf must be ten feet tall and from here, all I can focus on are its massive teeth poking out of its mouth. Then from below Raven's shout pulls me out of my shock. "Hey kid, snap out of it and jump down!" I don't even ask before I jump out of the tree and land on Raven's back with a thump.

She doesn't wait for me to recover from the fall before she takes off. I grab onto the saddle hard with my arms and legs, doing everything I can to stay astride her even grabbing hard onto her mane to keep me upright. It takes me a second but I gain my balance back. The wolf bays and begins its chase after us. Raven is running as fast as she can back towards camp. Back to Oak, back to my father.

"Raven, no!"

"What are you talking about? We need to get back to Oak and Silas or whatever that wolf thing is will kill us. We can't handle this on our own."

"We're going to have to fend for ourselves, Raven. We can't lead him straight to Father and Oak. They won't be ready for us and they'll be sitting ducks. Besides, we probably won't be able to outrun him all the way back to camp. Raven turns her head around to peek around at me mid-stride.

When she turns her head back she yells behind her, "Okay, kid, hang on."

Then before I know it we're diving left towards the creek. By the time we make the turn we're so far up the creek that in front of us it's wide and pelted with rocks and rapids.

I lean down on Raven's neck and yell over the wind ripping past us "Um, what are you doing, Raven?"

She yells back, "Just trust me."

I haven't ever trusted this horse in my life, but at this point, with a huge monster wolf chasing us down, I have no choice but to trust her. I grab on tighter with both my hands and legs twisting my hands through her thick mane.

As soon as Raven feels me bare down she picks up speed. I always knew Raven was faster than Oak, but I hadn't known how much faster. She's like a cheetah. It must be part of her being a Fae horse. No normal horse is this fast. The wind is whipping by me so fast it sends my hair flying and it's taking all my might to keep my eyes open, tears streaking down my face. Before I know what's happening, we're flying through the air.

She's trying to jump the creek? There's no way we're going to make it! But as fast as the thought enters my head it leaves because I peer towards the ground and realize we're already halfway across the creek. I don't know how she's doing this, but I thank the Gods she is. Raven lands on the opposite bank of the creek with plenty of room to spare.

When she lands, her momentum spins us around and we slide to a stop facing the creek, and the wolf's massive color fluid body is facing us, snarling. From here I can see the drool dripping off of his massive canines. His lips are pulled back in a menacing snarl so big I can see all of his teeth even up to his gums. He lets out a low huff and turns around walking back towards the forest he came out of. Then Raven spins away from the creek and takes off into the forest at top speed.

"What are you doing? He took off, he can't get over the river."

"Kid, did you see how big that thing is? I'm not taking any chances."

It takes about thirty seconds but then I hear it, a visceral howl and the ground trembles again.

"Um Raven?"

It sounds like the forest being ripped out by its roots.

"*Raven, run!*" I screech. We're running full out, but behind us it already sounds like the wolf is quickly catching up.

"We have to find somewhere to hide, there's no way we're going to outrun him."

"And what happens when we stop and he can smell us kid?"

"Crap."

I know I only have a few seconds before he catches us to figure out something to cover our scents so I lift my head and start searching around trying to find something, anything to help us. I search and search to no avail.

Then, as I'm deciding on a plan B, I spot a cave up ahead. It's far to our left and carved out of the side of a small hill. If I can slow down the wolf, we might have a chance of losing him and hiding in the back of it.

"Raven, I need to wound him so we can lose him, even just for a second, so I need you to slow down a bit and run as smoothly as you can."

"No way! Are you crazy? He'll catch us and eat us! I don't know about you, but I for one don't want to be wolf chow."

I pat the side of her neck, running my hand through her mane.

"Trust me," I say in my most reassuringly stern voice I can summon in the moment. "You asked me to trust you earlier, and I did. Now it's time for you to trust me."

I'm not sure how she does it without falling but she turns her head mid-stride again and looks me in the eye, probably weighing her options. I know she hasn't ever liked me so I know how hard it is for her to say the words that leave her mouth next.

"Just don't get us killed. Got that?"

"Got it! Okay the plan is I'll spin around on your back so I can shoot a few arrows into him and then, see that cave over there?" I say into her ear pointing towards the cave I spotted. "When I yell I want you to book it there as fast as you can. Now I'll be riding you off kilter still but don't worry about me, just get us there as fast as you can. Got it?"

"Got it," she says, sounding determined.

Raven slows her stride and her longer, slightly slower stride is so smooth I'm able to throw my left leg over the front of the saddle to the same side as my right. I try to pull out my bow but it's too awkward with the way I'm sitting, my quiver keeps bouncing on her shoulder and getting in the way of my bow. So I flip my right leg over her back so I'm sitting astride her facing backwards. From this angle all of the bouncing from my quiver stops and I can pull my bow from my back easily. I knock an arrow then refocus my vision to behold the huge, ungodly monster chasing us.

By now he's a lot closer than I thought he possibly could be. His claws scrape the ground leaving big divots in their wake, spraying dirt on all the trees behind him. I can even hear the dirt clods smacking destructively against the tree trunks behind him.

Our eyes meet and he lets out a grating howl, doubling his effort to get to us. It only takes a few strides before his gaping maw is a foot away from Raven's hind end. From here I can smell his foul, rotting, garbage smelling breath. I pull the string back on my bow until it goes taught between my fingers.

I aim and shoot.

Thump. Thump. Thump.

I shoot three arrows consecutively as fast as my arm will move, that warm sensation spreading back through my arms. I shoot two normal arrows and one of my mother's Fae hawk feathered arrows in rapid succession. One arrow goes through the side of the wolf's neck, the next goes through his shoulder, and the Fae arrow buries itself deeply in the beast's chest deeper than a normal arrow would have been capable of doing.

As soon as the last arrow lands I yell out "Go!"

We're lucky Raven is so quick reacting to my voice because as soon as she dives left the wolf rolls past where we were standing only seconds ago. After the arrows sink into his flesh, he takes a misstep and rolls head over tail, smashing trees as he goes.

Raven's speed puts some distance between wolf and us. I can hear the trees crashing behind Raven as the wolf rolls into them. I can't get my balance back while straddling Raven backwards so I lie down on her back and wrap my arms around her haunches. I hold on for dear life waiting for us to make it to the cave. She starts to slow and I roll off of her, landing in mud, square on my side. Landing so hard knocks the wind out of me but as soon as I can get air back into my lungs I push through the side pain and scramble to my feet.

When I stand back up, I see the cave. It's just a dark hole in the hillside. I was hoping it would be a big, deep hole where we could walk into and hide in the dark, but now, up close I can see the opening is so short I will have to bend to get in and the hole only goes back maybe twelve feet.

This is not good.

One person could hide in this cave but me and Raven? I'm not so sure.

I glance over to Raven. "You have to get in first. I'll try to help push you from behind, hurry".

"No, kid I can't fit, you need to get in. I can run and keep that beast away from you."

"No! That's a suicide mission. I will not hide without you

and that's it. Either you get in there or we leave together and that's final. Now hurry up!"

Raven shoots me a withering glare, but starts to crawl in. The mud around the cave entrance makes her slip and slide. The entrance is so short she has to crawl sideways and wiggle forward. I push her hind end, trying with all my might to help her get into the cave but she's too heavy; we're moving too slow. Mud starts coating both of us as we struggle.

Behind us I can hear the wolf whining and thrashing. I smile inside for a second knowing my arrows hit true and it hurt. I continue to push on Raven. My feet were sliding. This mud is making it impossible for me to get any traction. She's almost all the way in the cave when the whining and thrashing stop and an eerie quiet fills the air.

"Raven, we gotta move, come on girl"

"Attina I'm stuck. Run! Leave me! Get out of here please!"

I take in a deep breath. Grabbing my necklace I pray to the Gods, "Please give me the strength to do this, the strength to save her life". I yell out to Raven, "Let me try one more time and if we can't get you in there then I will turn around and protect you."

"No!" Raven bellows.

Sending up a silent prayer to the Gods, I steel myself and take a deep breath. I feel that warmth spreading throughout my body again and I feel like my insides are vibrating. I close off my hearing and take another steadying breath. I shut my eyes and ready myself to use all my strength on one more push. I let go of my necklace, putting both my hands on her flank before I heave one last time, and feel her move under me. I can't believe it.

At first I think my mind is playing tricks on me but then I open my eyes and see the ground moving under me. Then

I hear a grunt and she's on her feet inside the cave. Behind her I quickly dive into the dark with her. By now we're both covered head to toe in stinky mud; hopefully the smell of it will be enough to cover our scents.

The cave is dark but shallow. As soon as we get past the short threshold, the top of the cave opens up enough so I can sit atop Raven if I wanted to. Only an eerie silence can still be heard outside the cave. My eyes flick over to Raven and place my forefinger over my lips urging her to be quiet.

It takes a few seconds but then we hear it, a huge paw hammering the ground, stalking our way. I can hear the huffing sound of the wolf sniffing. I had hoped he would keep running in the direction we were running before but as he was falling he must have seen us take off to the left. I see his enormous paws, sharp razor-like claws and all, stalk slowly along the ground in front of the cave. I don't even want to think of the damage he could do with those things.

Following his nose, he continues across the front of the cave until he disappears from sight. Raven makes a move to walk to the front of the cave, but I put a hand against her chest, stopping her. She turns her head, glancing at me, a smile starting to spread over her features and I shake my head. I don't trust it. It was too easy to get away; even a normal wolf wouldn't give up so easily, let alone whatever that thing is.

We stand together in the dark for what seems like an eternity. Then I feel little clumps of dirt fall on my face. I wipe it away only for more dirt to land in my hair, a bigger clump this time. I gape up at the roof and see it's now raining down dirt. This can't be good.

A low growl drifts in from outside, it sounds like it's coming from the roof of the cave.

Great—this can't be good. Slowly, the wolf's face appears

in front of our cave from above. Up close, I can see his black face is scarred like someone burned him over and over and I again smell the rancid garbage-like stench coming from the drool dripping out of his mouth.

He snarls and snaps trying to force his face into the mouth of the cave, but the entrance is too small. Only his muzzle fits in and it's not enough to reach either Raven or me. He jumps down so he is standing in front of the cave opening and starts digging with his ginormous claws. The dirt falls away easily, the cave opening has no chance against those razor claws and neither do we.

"Um Raven, do you have a plan to get us out of this?" I say as I clasp at my necklace.

"No kid, I think we're done for once he gets through that wall, but it was a solid plan."

Raven moves closer to me and I drop my necklace and wrap both my arms tight around her neck, holding on to her for strength. At least we won't be alone when we meet our end.

All of a sudden I hear a war yell.

No not a yell, but a whinny. A noise I could imagine coming from a war-horse.

Raven whispers, "Oak."

Then I hear Father wail, *"Get away from them!"*

The wolf disappears from the front of the cave. I hear snarling, flesh and bone meeting steel, then a huge thump on the ground outside. I run out of the cave, not thinking of myself anymore. All I can think of is how Father and Oak must be laying on the ground in a pool of their own blood. I don't even think to knock an arrow in my bow before running out, every single bad scenario playing in rapid succession through my mind.

The sun is too bright for my eyes, so my hand raises to

cover them. As soon as they adjust, I see a giant wolf lying on the ground, bleeding out from a deep slice across its throat.

I feel the panic rising when I can't find Father or Oak. I scream "Father! Oak! Where are you?"

13

ATTINA

I HEAR MY FATHER'S LOUD CHUCKLE AND THEY BOTH STRIDE side by side out from behind the ginormous, limp wolf body. Father pats Oak on the neck laughing as he says, "Well that was fun old man. Almost made me feel young again, how about you?"

Oak's head bobs up and down as he replies, "Yes sir, it was great fun. Almost like running into battle again." There is something relaxed in both of their postures, which I haven't seen in years. Like defeating a monster took a huge weight off of their shoulders. Then Father sees me.

"Pumpkin!" he shouts, running over to me.

Then he goes to pick me up just like when I was a kid, but this time when he takes my weight he folds in half and drops down to his knees. I catch myself and fall down with Father, steadying him so he doesn't hit the ground too hard. Father's hand goes right to his side.

"What's wrong? What happened?"

I see his side and pull back. There is blood seeping through his shirt. I lift his shirt and it gets stuck on a sword I hadn't seen before, which is hanging from his side. Its pommel is in the shape of a fully bloomed rose but before I can analyze it more, I've got the shirt over his injury and my focus locks on three huge gashes across his side.

"Father you're hurt."

He snatches his shirt and pulls it back down chuckling. "Man, I thought he missed me, guess I was a tad too slow. I'm fine, pumpkin, it's not a big deal."

"It is a big deal; you're seriously hurt."

"I'm tougher than I look." He shoots me a wink, but the effect is unconvincing.

Then he sits up and puts his hands on either side of my face. His hands are firm and familiar which calms me, and he says, "Pumpkin, I'm fine. Are you okay? Not hurt? Where's Raven?" The concern in his voice breaks me.

He sits here so hurt, but is still more concerned about Raven and me than himself. The dam breaks and I start ugly crying, I hate showing any weakness, but around Father and our horses I feel safe enough. I still can't believe what just happened. Father wraps his arms around me and pulls me in close for a hug. In his soothing voice he says, "Aww, pumpkin, it's okay, it's just the adrenaline leaving your body. Where's Raven?"

At this point, I'm hiccupping from crying so violently I can only point towards the cave. Father releases me and runs to the cave but Oak, my old faithful, takes up his position and lets me lean against his shoulder for comfort. While I stand there getting my emotions under control, I scan over to the huge dead wolf monster.

In death, its fur stuck to one color, it is a deep black, almost like a void in the landscape. I walk over to the limp dead body and touch its pelt. Its coat is rough and sticky and when I smell my hand it smells like rotting flesh, but how is such a thing possible this creature hasn't been dead five minutes. It couldn't already be rotting. Could it? So what is with the smell?

I walk around its body searching for my arrows but they're nowhere to be found, he must have ripped them out before he found us hiding in the cave. When I walk over to his face, it's stuck in a growl with its lips pulled up over its teeth. His tongue in death is purple and hangs out of its mouth onto the ground in a puddle of bright red blood, which leaks from the massive gash across its throat. The gash is so deep you can see the wolf's white, blood splattered spine. Father must have been furious to drive his blade across the wolf's throat so severely.

It takes a while, but Father digs Raven out of the cave and after a short break we start the ride back to camp. On the way back, I ride Oak, Father happily rides Raven, and everything feels right again.

I peek over at Father and I can't seem to keep my eyes off of the sword hanging at his side. "Where did you get that?"

Father glances at me and then scans his eyes to where my eyes are focused and a small smile spreads across his face as he turns back forward he says, "It was your mother's".

My eyes widen in shock as I quietly whisper, "What the fuck," to myself.

I take a better look at the sword. I didn't realize how stunning the hilt was earlier when I saw it on Father. It has a rose in full bloom and the hand guard is made of metal vines complete with thorns pointing out away from the wielder's hand. Engraved down the blade of the sword are some sort of symbols I haven't seen before in any of the books I've ever read, but they're beautiful. They flow and glide over the blade, the symbols so finely crafted into the weapon you almost lose yourself in where the engraving stops and the sword itself begins. It is an absolutely stunning weapon and knowing it was my mother's makes the sword even more special.

"Why did she leave it with you? It's gorgeous, it must have been extremely important to her."

He turns and peers at me, sadness coating his features, then sighs. "She wasn't sure what would happen to her when she went back to her father and she wanted to make sure this sword was passed down to you when you were strong enough. She figured leaving it with me would be the safest way to guarantee you would get it one day."

Staring down at the sword I focus on those black, winding, flowing symbols. "What do the symbols mean?"

Father glances back to the sword then to me. "Your mother said they meant 'moonlight reveals all shadows.' She said it was a reminder to her, but she didn't ever really explain what they reminded her of."

I let that sink in. Then, I ask what has been poking at the back of my mind. "How did you and Oak know where to find us?"

Oak turns his head to gape up at me and says, "You really think we didn't hear that monster? I knew what area you would most likely be in from all our years hunting together and from there we followed the huge paw tracks."

Raven laughs out. "And we both figured taking that monster back to camp would just put you guys in danger. I guess we were wrong."

Father breathes out heavily. "Well, we didn't get out of there unscathed so I'm glad we were able to sneak up on him. Things might have turned out worse if you'd brought that werewolf back to camp. Attina, you know that's what the monster was, right?"

I glance at Father with what must be confusion written

on my face because Father squints down at Raven. "You didn't tell her?"

Raven huffs and snottily replies, "We didn't have time for a heart to heart, sorry."

He ignores her haughty remark and turns to me. "That was a werewolf; a hunter for the Fae King. Your mother told me when the King has top secret missions he doesn't even want his top slayers to know about, he sends one of these werewolves."

"Wait so that thing was a Fae creature? That explains it's strangeness."

Both horses turn to peer up at me, which makes blood rush to my cheeks. I backpedal, "Oh I didn't mean you two––I just meant—"

Oak turns his head back forward "we know what you meant. It's okay, most Fae creatures are strange."

Father continues, "Yes, and obviously that bastard knew someone was out here or he wouldn't have sent a werewolf. I don't know how, but he seems to know more than we think he does. The upside of this whole thing is now he's shown his cards a little. He must think something here is a serious threat or he wouldn't have sent the werewolf. Now we need to head back to camp, pack some essentials, and get back to town."

"Why? Are we going home for good now?"

"No, I need to get you the map to Sanctuary, the place where the rest of the town went to, just in case something like this happens again and we aren't so lucky the next time around." Then he grabs his side making a pained noise and bending over in pain.

I gasp out worriedly, "Are you okay?"

Father sucks in air through his clenched teeth and eyes

me before sitting up and plastering, what I know is one of his fake smiles, on his face.

"Yeah, Pumpkin I'll be fine. I just need you to sew me back up."

We sit in silence for the rest of the ride back to camp, both adrift in our own little worlds. Besides worrying about my Father's wound, I am thinking of everything I've learned. It worries me. Obviously, Henrik knows I exist. Why would he bother sending such a monster after a half-breed like me? Why am I so special to rate such an extreme measure? Does he know my mother wanted me to take over his kingdom? How could I scare him so bad? A girl with little to no power should not scare him enough to warrant a werewolf being sent to kill her. The only answer I can come up with is he's a madman and there is no use in trying to understand a madman.

It takes longer to get back to camp than I thought it would. We ran a lot farther than I thought possible, just more of a testament to how fast Raven is. When we finally do make it back, Father gingerly dismounts, grunting and groaning the entire way down. Then he calls to me, "Attina get over here." I dismount and walk around Oak, petting his cheek as I walk. Father unbuckles the sword from his side and he holds it out to me.

"I want you to carry this and get used to the weight of it. I was going to give this to you after we finished your training, but you definitely proved yourself today."

I reach out for my mother's prized possession and start tearing up. "Thank you Father, this means the world to me. I will cherish it forever."

He smiles and says, "No reason to tear up. I was tired of lugging it around anyway and besides it's kind of embarrassing having such an obviously girly sword strapped to my side, it's hard to look manly wielding it."

That does it. I start laughing through the tears along with him. He knows what to say to make me laugh, no matter what, without fail.

I smile at him. "Okay, manly man, just tell me what you want to take with us, you're in no shape to be carrying anything." I glance over to Father and now his smile reaches his eyes.

"Thank you, pumpkin" he says. "We need to take only the essentials like I said, so basically just our medical kit, weapons, some water, and some food."

"Okay, just point and I'll grab." As I'm saying this, I strap on my mother's sword—no *my* sword—to my hip. The baldric feels like it was made for me. The dark leather is soft and hugs my body exactly where it should, so the sword feels weightless on me. You would think the scabbard banging against my hip and thigh would be annoying, but in reality, it feels comforting even though I haven't ever wielded a sword for real, in my life. I mean I've chopped at a tree with one but that's about it.

Father sits down on one of the logs by our fire pit and points out the few things we'll need. After I've grabbed these things, I open our meager med kit and wrap Father's wound as best I can with it, hoping it holds for the ride home. Then I help Father up and walk him back to Raven.

"Raven can you kneel down, please?"

Raven kneels on the ground and we both help Father get back on.

"Okay, hold on to the horn and give me your foot." I see him grab onto the saddle horn and I lift, giving him a boost to get him in the saddle again. Raven gets back up as slow as she can to keep from jostling him, but I see Father still cringe in pain. I load our few items in Raven and Oak's saddle bags then climb back on top of Oak.

Father turns Raven around and we start the ride back towards home.

I take one last scan of our campsite and then bend down and pat Oak. "Okay, old man let's go home, we'll be back here soon enough."

"Yes, you're right. Let's get going my lady, it's a long ride home."

14

———

ATTINA

THE TRIP HOME GOES MUCH QUICKER THAN THE TRIP TO CAMP, even with Father hurt. Raven and Oak are less weighed down with only us and the essentials on their backs, so now they can both move faster, and it only takes us a full day to get home this time.

When we get home, I help Father off of Raven then I unsaddle the horses while he goes inside the house to wait for me to tend to his wounds. When I get done unsaddling, I brush down both of our horses and give them fresh food and water before heading inside.

As I walk into the house, I can hear Father sucking in breaths deep and loud. He must be in much more intense pain than I thought. I walk into his room, his shirt and the bandage is off and he has a small towel pressed against his side. His blood is already seeping through the white towel, coloring it a deep red.

"Let me look," I say walking across his bedroom towards him.

I kneel down next to his bed and pull off the towel, now seeing the damage fully. The whole right side of his torso is all red but that's not the bad part. The bad part is the three deep cuts across his side have yellow puss barely starting to crawl away from the edges.

"I have to see how deep these are," Before Father has a chance to answer, I push open the cuts and Father grunts in agony.

"It looks like the claws missed anything vital, thank the Gods, so I'm going to clean out the puss and then you'll need stitches."

With a pained expression on his face Father says, "I swear those claws barely touched me."

"We're lucky it wasn't worse then."

I pat my Father's knee, stand up, and head to the kitchen to get all of the supplies I'll need. I pull out our full first aid kit and then go to the cabinet and take out our whiskey bottle. Father received it, as a present, years ago, and he only uses it to take a shot to "burn out a cold" as he calls it. The bottle is still almost full. I grab everything I'll need and walk back into Father's room. He's already starting to look pale from the pain. I hand him over the whiskey bottle.

"Take a few drags on this, fixing you up is going to hurt, *a lot*."

Father doesn't even say a word before quickly snatching the bottle out of my hand and taking a few big swigs. While Father gets to numbing himself, I start preparing everything I'll need to fix the deep gouges in his side. Thank the Gods James taught me how to stitch people up when I was younger. I think back to when he first taught me how to do stitches.

One day when we were kids, we were out exploring, and I fell down. Me falling down was not out of the ordinary but of course with my luck, this time I landed on a sharp stick. The stick jammed into my leg and gave me a huge deep cut which needed stitches. James, perpetually the teacher, showed me how to do stitches while he was working on stitching me up. I think it was probably more to keep my mind off of the pain, but I did learn a valuable skill.

Then over the years people in the town sporadically got hurt and needed stitches, and James and I would help out stitching people up, so I know I can handle stitching up my Father. By the time I have everything set up, my Father is already a little woozy. I can tell because he's sitting up on the edge of his bed swaying a little, so before I lose my nerve to work on him I get down to business.

"Okay, you can lay down now." Father lies down and I pull his belt out from the loops of his pants, fold it in half and hand it to him. "You might want to bite down on it, this is really going to hurt." I take the whiskey from his hands and say, "Brace yourself, I need to disinfect the wound and get all of this puss out," before I pour the whiskey all over his wounds.

I splash the brown liquid all over his side making sure to get it all the way deep into his cuts. He gasps for air and starts shaking from the pain the alcohol causes. I take a clean cloth and press it to the wound.

The contact on the wound must be too much because Father bends up in a half sit-up and lets out a huge breath of air. He tries to wiggle away from the cloth until I give him a glare to say I won't put up with such nonsense, then pull the cloth off and give him a few seconds to compose himself.

"Okay, we need to do that one more time to make sure we got out all the bad stuff, so take in a deep breath and I'll count to three."

I pull out a clean cloth and start my count.

"One..."

I unscrew the lid on the whiskey bottle.

"Two…"

And I throw the whiskey all over his wound.

Father yells, "Damn it, Attina! You said on the count of three!"

I press the new, clean cloth back on top of the wounds as I repeat what he told me the first day of our training. "Assume nothing, and trust no one." Then I wink at him. "Besides, we got it over with didn't we? And this way you didn't have a chance to tense up." I dab the cloth over the cleaned wounds, getting rid of as much moisture as possible before I get to stitching him up. He lies down and closes his eyes. His breathing becomes deeper and steadier as I begin working on him.

Halfway through stitching him up I ask, "Okay where did you put the map to Sanctuary before you pass out?"

My Father chuckles, "You're going to laugh at this one; it's in a super secret place—I shoved it under my bed."

I stop stitching for a second and glance at him, shocked, and then I roll my eyes at him.

"I don't know if that's stupid or genius. It's such an obvious spot it would either be the first spot checked, or it wouldn't get checked at all. Well, let's finish getting you stitched up and we'll switch you to my bed, I'll change the wet sheets on your bed and grab the map. Tonight, since your bed is soaked in whiskey I'll just sleep on the couch and if you need me, you can just yell."

"Thank you so much, pumpkin. I don't know what I would ever do without you."

My eyes flick to Father and I crack a smile. "Crash and burn."

We both chuckle until Father moans in pain and grasps at his side. I finish stitching him up, and wrap his wound in cloth to keep out any dirt or crud. I have to help Father to my bed. He's still a little woozy from all the whiskey he downed earlier. I drop him, gently, in my bed and sit down next to him to tuck him in. I move to leave but just as I start moving, I hear his voice.

"Attina, I don't think I've ever told you this before, but you are the greatest thing to ever happen to me."

"Oh, stop it." I wave him away. "That's just the whiskey talking. Now get some rest mister." I stand to leave the room and just as I turn Father grabs me by my arm, stopping me.

"No, I mean it! You've grown into such a beautiful, capable woman. I am so proud of who you've become. You can hunt and shoot, you're smart and funny, and you're loving and generous. I couldn't be a prouder father."

Those words hit me in the heart fiercely. I feel tears creeping out of my eyes. Why the hell am I crying so much lately damnit? Never in my life have I been a crier.

"That means so much to me. Thank..."

Then I realize he's laid his head down, passed out, snoring. I smile to myself, wipe the tears from my eyes, and cover him up with my blanket. I absolutely need to stop crying, this is getting ridiculous.

Before I leave the room, I can hear his deep snore. His snoring is ear-splitting. All my life I've raced to get to sleep before he did, but this time when I get to my door I turn around and smile. After everything that's happened these past few days, his snoring is incredibly comforting.

I walk back to Father's room and strip off the soiled blankets and sheets. I take them outside and put them in the wash bin then head back inside to find the map. I pull back the mattress cushion and the map is right under where my Father's head would lay. Surprisingly the map isn't much, only a simple sheet of parchment folded in half. I walk it into the living room and slide it down into the pocket of my quiver for safekeeping, then head outside to take care of Father's bedding before the blood stains set.

When I get back inside, I grab my quiver, pull out the map and flop down on the couch to read its contents. When I unfold it I see it's a roughly drawn map and I can tell by the writing that Father drew it.

At the extreme left of the map is our town; a little way up from there and to the right is marked as our camp site. Then way up at the top, a little to the right from our town is Shadow Mountain. On the map you can tell it is a massive mountain and my Father must have not actually known how big the mountain was because he drew it on the edge of the paper so the top of the mountain is missing.

Down and far to the right of our town is a site marked Sanctuary. It's way off by itself, past the other three towns I know about, Hugyo, Salhay and Fedum. To get there we will have to pass through those towns but at least we will be able to restock necessities along the way.

It will be a long hard journey but with Father and Oak by my side, I know we can make it to Sanctuary. As I drift off to sleep I absentmindedly wonder if the people in those towns followed our townspeople on their journey to Sanctuary.

15

———

ATTINA

The next morning, I wake early to an empty house. I get out of bed, dress, walk over to the corner of my room, and snatch up my bow and quiver. I hurry outside in search of Father. When I make it outside the horses are already both kneeling down fully saddled. Father walks gingerly out of our shed carrying a saddle bag in each hand. He's moving a lot slower today and his eyes are bloodshot; I guess he's hungover from all the whiskey he drank last night.

I shout at him, "What do you think you're doing!"

My yell startles him, and he drops the saddle bags.

"I'm just grabbing a couple of fresh supplies for the ride back to camp."

"For the ride back? Did you hit your head last night after all that whiskey? You need to be in bed! Didn't you see all those stitches I had to put in you?"

I walk over to him and grab him by his arm to guide him back to our house.

"Now let's get you back to bed, you need some rest. Besides, I won't be too happy if you tear those stitches and I have to sew you up again. I don't even want to know how you saddled those horses without blowing them out."

He yanks his arm away from me, picking up the saddle-bags before walking over to the horses.

"No, Attina. We can't be around town more than absolutely necessary."

"What are you talking about?"

"Pumpkin, last night when we showed up here, I remembered you should be coming into your Awakening any day now. We can't be around our town when it happens. I'm not completely sure what your mother meant by the ground quaking. I don't know how massive a reaction it will be. For all I know, your Awakening could rip cracks in the earth, and I don't want you to accidentally destroy the town."

"Oh..." I whisper as I stare at my feet, realizing he's right. We don't know for sure what will happen and if the world shakes from an Awakening then the town could shake so hard it falls to the ground.

I look over to him and say, "But what about your stitches? You can't ride like that," pointing at his hurt side.

He glances down at his side then looks to the saddle bags in his hands and continues as he lays one bag on top of Oak.

"I did think of that already and I loaded up both of our saddle bags with better medical supplies, everything you'll need for stitching me back up; some whiskey included." He says this last part while winking at me.

I laugh. "Okay just let me get a fresh pair of clothes on and we'll get on the road." I move to walk back into the house and hear him shout after me.

"Hurry, pumpkin. No longer than absolutely necessary, remember?" I lift my hand over my head and wave to say yeah okay or F off. I'm not sure which.

I head into my room for a change of clothes and to pack another bag. I'd only brought a few items when we first left town but now it seems like this camping trip will be for the foreseeable future, so I better take more clothes with me while I have the chance. Most of my clothes were made out of wool from town livestock so I grab a little of everything, lots of layers I can use throughout the winter if necessary.

Then I strap my mother's sword around my hips before grabbing my quiver and bow as I walk out my door to the back door of the house. As I put my right hand on the door-knob, I turn around to stare once more at the house I grew up in, trying to save every detail safely in my mind, not knowing when the next time I'll see this place is. I get the sudden urge to walk over to our fireplace.

Over the fireplace is one lone picture. There is a family photo of my dad my mother, and me. The only picture I've ever seen of my mother and she is holding me. I must be only a couple of weeks old in this picture. I'm so tiny. My mother is cradling me in her arms staring down at me and on her face I can see the immense love and joy written there. Gazing at the picture of our little family, it hits me again how much I look like my mother.

My eyes obviously came from my father but every other feature on my face is the spitting image of my mother. She has long wavy beautiful brown hair. I haven't ever thought of my hair as beautiful, but seeing it on my mother I know now it's truly comely. Our full cheeks and small, slight button nose finishes out her face. Behind her, Father has his arms wrapped around Mother's stomach and under her arms, so it appears like he's holding both of us at the same time. On his face is the biggest smile I've ever seen him wear, I can see how proud he is of his little family and I can see the love he has for us beaming out through his eyes.

Tears start to fill my eyes. I wish I could remember a time when we were all together, and a time where Father was this happy. Throughout the years he's been happy, but without fail, I could tell in all those happy moments he was heartbroken my mother wasn't there to share them with him. Here, in this picture his expression is pure bliss. That urge returns to take hold of me and tells me to take the picture with me. The thought of leaving the picture here kick starts a pain in my chest like someone's hand is in my chest squeezing my heart.

I follow my heart and without thinking grab the frame and shove it in my quiver pocket right next to the map to Sanctuary. I take one last circle around the living room and then head out the back door to meet Father and the horses. Father has already made it atop Raven and everyone is just standing there waiting for me, Father is the first one to say anything.

"We were getting worried about you. Are you ready, pumpkin?"

I nod my head and throw my quiver and bow over my shoulder while I walk over to Oak. I give his big, trunk-sized head a pat and then end up wrapping my arms around it. Oak pushes his head against my chest, and I hear Father next to us, "Okay guys, we need to get going." I give Oak one more big squeeze, and with my sword strapped to my side, clumsily climb up into the saddle.

The ride back to camp is slow going since Father is so sore from me stitching him up, but it should only take us about a day and a half to get back to camp this time. After the first day on the trail, I have to stitch him back up in a couple spots but nothing too dramatic.

The next day it takes most of the day for me to gather the courage to ask a question which has been on my mind off and on since I was a little kid, but I do eventually gather enough courage to ask.

"Hey, Father, can I ask you a question?" I call to him from behind, where I'm riding Oak.

"Always, pumpkin," Father calls over his shoulder on top of Raven.

"How did you and my mother meet?"

"Get up here and I'll tell you; I don't want to shout!" He calls to me.

I air kiss at Oak, and he picks up his pace to a trot until we are walking side by side with Raven and Father. He turns his head to me, smiles, and then starts his story.

"I guess it makes sense you want to know how we met. Any kid would want to know something like that even if their mother wasn't Fae. You must be sitting on pins and needles."

"What are you talking about? You know I've wanted to know all about you and my mother forever. It's not solely because she was Fae, I just never asked because I figured what was the point when you wouldn't ever talk to me about her anyway," I snap.

Father's face turns sad, and I instantly regret the way I snapped at him. "Father...I'm—" I stutter out.

He doesn't let me finish and merely talks over me. "I'm sorry for all those years I kept you in the dark about your mother. I probably could have handled it better, but I did the best I could."

I trot Oak in front of Raven and stop, making sure Father pays attention to what I have to say. I look him in the eye. "You were and are the greatest father in the world. You had to be a mother and a father. I know I wasn't the easiest child to raise, but I wouldn't change the way I was raised for the world. I would have loved for Mother to have been around growing up but don't ever think I was wanting for anything growing up. You showed and continue to show me enough love and support for two parents— I love you." By now I am choking up trying hard not to cry for what feels like the fourteenth time this trip.

Father looked me in the eye throughout my entire speech but his face was like a rock while I was talking. Now that I've finished his face softens and he smiles. "I love you too, pumpkin. So you want to know how your mother and I met? Let's get moving and I'll tell you whatever you want to know from now on. Promise."

I smile and nod. "Okay, let's go." I turn Oak back in the direction of camp and we all resume our journey.

"Your mother and I met on the Day of Destruction," he starts nonchalantly.

I hold up a hand "Wait! Wait! You mean you're older than the Day of Destruction? That was *ages* ago." I smile slyly.

Peeking over to Father I see him roll his eyes "Har-de-har. Very funny, Attina. Can I continue now?" he says while pointedly staring at me.

"Yes, sorry I couldn't help myself" I apologize chuckling to myself. "What were you doing there anyway?"

"I was actually a guard. Remember the story I told you as a child about what happened on the Day of Destruction?"

"Yes," I answer absentmindedly.

"Well, the proprietor, Wharton, was my boss. I was hired as his personal guard, but he used me more as an assistant."

My tone turns grave as I say, "So, um, I guess you were kind of fired since the proprietor ended up dying that night."

"It's not as easy as all that baby girl. Like I said he used me as more of an assistant so that night Wharton sent me to oversee his workers and make sure everything went off without a hitch, but you know what ended up happening. After the Fae started pouring out of Shadow Mountain I ran back to Wharton's office but by the time I made it there your mother was standing over his dead body covered in his blood. As I walked in she turned to me and her fiery eyes found mine."

"So, wait, did you two fight?" I interrupt.

"Well, if you'd let me finish you would have already found out the answer to that question."

"Sorry, I'll be quiet." Heat rises to my cheeks. I seriously can't seem to stay quiet right now. I want to know everything.

"We did not fight, and honestly to this day I still don't understand why. Our eyes met and I don't know how to explain it, but something clicked between us. I had a visceral reaction to seeing her like I was looking at someone I'd known my whole life. I walked over to her and she lowered her sword and in a bewitching voice said, 'well hello you,' and ran over to me, jumped into my arms like we had been together forever. Everything just clicked. Before we knew what was really happening, your mother and I were climbing on Oak together and the four of us were running away from our commitments and our previous lives to make a new life together."

"Wait. I don't understand. You said the four of us but you only mentioned three names."

"Yes. Your mother, me, Oak, and Raven."

"Wait. Okay I know Oak was my mother's war-horse, but why were you there Raven? You had to have been so young."

Raven snorts. "You can answer that one, Silas."

Father laughs. "Haha okay. Well first, you must know Raven has perpetually been incredibly ornery. She was supposed to stay in the stables that night, but *somebody* was not about to be told what to do. She wanted to follow her father into battle. So, she snuck out and did just that."

I glance from Oak to Raven throwing my hands up in exasperation. "Wait. Oak, you're Raven's father? Why didn't you ever tell me?"

"You never asked," Oak answers nonchalantly like it's no big deal.

I am about to retort, but as I open my mouth, our camp materializes into view.

16

ATTINA

When we make it back to camp, Raven immediately kneels down to make it easier for Father to get off. Like usual, Father doesn't show an iota of weakness as he dismounts but I can tell he is still extremely sore so I help him sit down by the fire pit before checking his stitches.

When I get a chance to inspect the stitches they're red and angry, he winces when I touch around the wound, but the stitches seem to be holding just fine. The sun is setting so I get a fire started for him and start taking care of the things which need done right away in camp.

I start putting away the things Father put in our saddle bags and then begin unsaddling the horses before I leave to find wood for the night. I get Oak unsaddled, brushed down, and settled in the open meadow by camp for his evening meal. Then I move to Raven to start unsaddling her but as I grab for her cinch she moves away slightly. I stare at her confused.

"You have to collect and split wood still right?" Raven asks.

"Well yeah after I get you unsaddled and brushed down."

Raven moves back towards me, walking to my side so I can climb in her saddle if I wanted.

"Well, why don't we both collect wood today? It'll go faster if you're on my back and I can also help carry wood back."

Without saying anything I pick up my bow and arrows, strap them on again and swing my body up into the saddle. The only thing I still haven't figured out is how to effortlessly get into a saddle with a sword strapped to my side. So, getting on Raven is awkward, but I make it on, barely.

I wave to Father as we walk out of camp and behind me I yell, "We'll be back! We're going to get firewood." I don't hear a reply so I glance over my shoulder and my father is still sitting where I left him watching us leave with a big smile on his face. I turn around to face forward as Raven and I head back into the woods.

I scan around us and I feel so at peace. I feel like this is where my soul belongs, in the middle of nowhere, in the woods, with my father's horse and my mother's sword on my hip. The birds are chirping, and the air feels fresh and cool against my exposed skin, the smell is so crisp and inviting.

I take in a deep calming breath but then Raven stops moving without warning. I automatically climb off of her without really thinking. I walk in front of her searching for a downed tree or something I can break down into smaller pieces for firewood, but when I take a scan, I see nothing but big green healthy trees.

I turn back to Raven and see her staring at the ground with her head hanging low, dejected. I walk over to her and I put my hands on either side of her soft baby doll head.

"What's wrong, Raven?"

"I feel terrible and I'm sorry."

I drop my hands and take a step back staring into her eyes, "What do you mean? What's going on with you?"

"I've been incredibly awful to you over the years. I'm so sorry. I was just a babe when I was around your mother and I just completely idolized her. I've been thinking about her and how I've treated you over the years, and I finally realized how horrible I've been to you. Your whole life I've expected you to live up to my skewed version of your mother. An image, which would be impossible for even your mother to live up to, I'm sure. I hope you can find it in your heart to forgive me." And then she looks up at me with a sadness behind her expectant eyes.

"Raven, growing up I wanted so badly to be your best friend, that wasn't the way things worked out, but there's nothing to forgive. I understand completely, and I just hope one day I can call you my friend and partner."

Raven bends her head down. "Thank you. Nothing would make me happier than to be that for you, my lady".

The words "my lady" confuse me. Oak's called me the same name ever since I first found out he could talk, but it sounds normal coming from him. Coming from Raven it sounds like the words hold more meaning, they seem heavy, like they carry weight with them. I pet Raven on her forehead and walk back to the saddle and climb on without saying anything more. We start our search for firewood again. We walk for a while and that's when I notice it—the silence. All the birds have stopped chirping.

"Raven, do you hear that?"

Her ears perk up and rotate around, listening. "It's too quiet. The birds vanished." Both of our heads are on a swivel now, but we don't see anything out of the ordinary. I begin to worry at my necklace, moving it back and forth along its chain, my nerves getting the best of me. I don't think it's safe for us to be out here alone anymore, I seriously don't want to run into another werewolf.

I lean down and ask, "Lets head back to camp. Better to be safe than sorry. What do you think?" Raven immediately nods her head and effortlessly spins around.

On our walk back, I'm completely on edge. I'm straining my ears, hoping and praying to the Gods to hear any animal out in the forest and for everything to be okay. Raven hasn't said a word but I can feel the tension radiating off of her from under the saddle. It feels like I'm riding a stiff tree trunk instead of a fleshy horse.

I hear Raven nervously murmur, "We have enough wood to get us through the night anyway."

"Yeah, there's no real reason we need to be out here this late," I say trying to reassure myself.

Then I hear that war cry again. The same one I heard when the werewolf was trying to get at me and Raven in the cave. Raven stops moving.

At the same time we both breath out, "Oak."

I scream, "Let's go!" and kick Raven in her sides as hard as I can to knock her out of her shock. She rears and takes off like we are being chased by the Gods themselves. She's running with every bit of energy she has, and I'm pushing her harder and harder the whole way. When we reach the edge of camp, everything is pure chaos.

The whole camp is smashed, shattered, and on fire. Our things are strewn all around the forest, and our tents are even hanging from trees now. The lighted logs from the fire I started for Father are strewn all over the place catching the ground and forest on fire.

How could this have happened?

I hear a woman scream at the top of her lungs right

before I see Oak flying through the air out of the forest. He slams hard into a tree on the edge of camp. I hear the distinctive crunching of bone before Raven and me both scream Oak's name at the top of our lungs.

Before I can process anything, Raven has us next to Oak and I've somehow gotten off her and I'm kneeling on the ground next to him. He's lying unmoving in the grass at the base of the tree he was thrown against. I put my hands on Oaks neck, stroking him gently, praying to the Gods he can survive this attack. Then he coughs and crimson blood trickles out of his mouth. As soon as he feels my hands touch his fur he shudders in pain and tries to scoot away from me.

"Oak, old man, it's me Attina, it's okay I'm here."

I stroke his neck in the softest, most calming way possible, putting every bit of healing energy into him as I can. Oak opens his big cream-colored eyes and he visibly relaxes.

"My lady," he chokes out, his eyes are soft like he's happy to see me.

He tries to get up but only makes it up to a sitting position. Then as if he's smacked with reality he glances quickly between Raven and I. Behind us I hear the woman's scream again. She sounds like a wounded animal howling for its life.

"What are you two doing here?" Oak shouts over the screaming woman.

"We came back to help you and Father."

But Oak is no longer speaking to me. Anger coats his features. His brow crinkles, and his eyes sharpen and darken as he glares directly into Raven's eyes.

"Do your duty, damn it!"

This confuses me. I search between them scanning their faces for an answer. "What?" But no one is paying attention to what I have to say. Oak and Raven are in their own world.

Oak screams, "Take our future queen away right now! Why would you bring her into this kind of danger?"

The woman wails again and then there's an explosion. It sounds like a tree is shattering. Oak turns towards the sound then back to Raven.

"Leave now! It's Titania."

But Raven seems to have gone into shock again. She can't take her eyes off of Oak. Another tree explodes in the distance and then I hear Father's yell from behind me. I turn and see him race behind a tree, I assume, to hide from the woman. Before Oak or Raven can say anything or stop me, I race toward Father, pulling my bow from my back knocking an arrow as I move.

"Father!" I yell, running with everything I have wildly towards him.

He leaves his hiding spot and limps from one tree to the next, dragging a sword behind him. Holding his stitched side, which is now a deep crimson, he turns my way. His eyes grow big and he seems shocked to see me. The tree he limped out from behind just seconds ago, explodes.

Time seems to stand still as I see my father thrown through the air; huge hunks of wood flying after him. The chunks flying through the air are as big as a fully-grown man and look like sharpened spears, searching for a target to embed into.

Father lands hard on the ground ten feet from me. I can hear his body smashing onto the earth with a wet, sucking, bone-crunching noise. I start moving, running to his aid, but on the edge of my vision, where the now exploded tree used to be, I see movement. I make it to Father's side as I glance towards the movement and lock eyes with a woman.

This has to be the woman Oak spoke of. This must be Titania.

The woman, who rambles towards us, is more like a wild uncaged animal than any human I've ever seen. She might have once been beautiful, but such a time is long gone. Her clothes are hanging in tatters and caked in dirt. Her visible skin is covered in abrasions, with dried blood everywhere. Her hair is a tangled mess. It seems like at one time her hair was long, brown, and beautiful, but not anymore. Now her hair hangs in dreadlocks down to her waist. Her eyes are what shock me the most. They are a blazing red. The fire catching around camp is reflected in those red eyes, which only makes them shimmer more, like the fires of hell itself are bursting out of them.

She locks eyes with me and wails. Not a scream anymore, but a pained wail like flesh is being ripped from her. I pull my bow string and let my knocked arrow fly. Its aim true until she grabs it out of the air right before it impales her in the chest. She cocks her head stares at the arrow in her hand like it's something foreign to her. Then she glances back at me, I grab another arrow, but by the time I grasp it the woman has made it over to me, faster than the blink of an eye, and grabs my throat.

I take the arrow in my hand and shove it deep into the arm seizing my throat. She screams and knocks me down onto my back, the bow flying from my hands. I move to grab my sword from my side but as I fall, I land on top of it and now it's useless, it might as well be miles away. I reach for the hilt anyway, but by the time I touch it, the woman is on top of me pinning my arms down. She lifts her arm and now I see her long sharp claws ready to rip out my throat. I flinch and close my eyes, waiting for her to dig her claws deep into my chest in a vicious attack, which I'm sure will kill me.

I wait and wait, but nothing happens. I open my eyes and can see her confused face a mere breath length away from my face. But she's not looking at me. She's staring at my necklace. When she threw me on the ground my necklace popped out from under my shirt and now the woman is just staring at it, completely entranced.

Then, like a blur, my father jumps from over my head and tackles the woman off of me. I sit up and I see he's holding the woman with her arms pulled behind her. The woman is snapping and biting like a rabid animal, but then our eyes lock and I feel something align inside of me and immediately a pain rocks through me like nothing I've felt before.

Over the years I've split my legs open, broken bones, and almost frozen to death, but nothing I've been through so far compares to the pain I'm in now. I roll over and try to stand up but I can only make it to my knees and elbows before my body gives out on me. My head presses against the ground as my body begins to shake uncontrollably.

As the world begins to sway from the pain, I snatch at the ground trying to hold on to anything to make the world stop spinning. I can hear Father yelling for me but it sounds like he's a world away.

The sky above me starts to cloud over as I fall to my side. The ground has started to shake violently, and I can't keep my balance anymore. I manage to focus on my father who is holding the woman in a death grip, swaying around from her struggling and the violent quake of the earth. I can tell he's losing his grasp on her. She's too strong and the quakes are making it impossible for him to keep a hold on her.

Any second now I just know she will break free of him and kill all of us and there's nothing I can do to stop it. I lay there searching around desperately for anything to help me save everyone I love. I see a huge, splintered chunk of wood sticking up out of the ground a couple of feet in front of the woman. If my father or I could only push her down on top of that stake we could at least get away far enough to lose her and save our skins.

I can't move, I'm in so much pain, no matter how much I want to shove that stake through her heart, I can't. I start picturing it in my mind anyway. Me pushing her with a hard thud, the sound of the spike sliding and squelching through her body, her sprawling out on top of it and the wood poking out of her body, giving us the time to run. I imagine it over and over in my mind until that's all I am. I'm not lying on the ground writhing in pain, I'm pushing the woman down onto that stake.

I see movement out of the corner of my eye, but I ignore it. All I can focus on is killing the woman. The rage rises in me along with the pain; the rage makes dealing with the pain tolerable, so I hold on to it with everything in my being. I feel my blood throbbing between my ears, my brain feels like it's about to explode from the excruciating pain filling my body and the incessant beating of blood between my ears. With all this rising pain I feel a force rise right alongside it.

I peek up and lock eyes with my father. His face has fallen, and his shoulders are drawn in. His eyes are wide and panicked, but the pain in those eyes of his breaks the tentative hold I have on my emotions. I close my eyes and scream from the pain coursing through me and from the frustration in the realization there is nothing I can do to fix this. In the back of my mind, I sense some force inside me awakening quick as an arrow.

When I glance over, I notice the stake has started to shake drastically in the ground. Then in an instant the stake is gone, and I hear the sound of skin ripping apart and blood squirting. Once the noise hits my ears it feels like a weight is lifted off of my chest. I'm still in immense pain, but now I can lift my head and I'm able to get my own unrestrainable screaming under control. The next instant I see Father's scared face in front of mine. He's holding my face between his hands.

"Attina, Attina are you okay?"

I glance up to him and shake my head. I am definitely not okay. My body feels like it's about to burst apart. I can't even talk, but if I could talk, I would ask him to knock me out so I wouldn't have to be awake for all this pain. I don't know if me shaking my head registers with him since the world is shaking so violently, but the look in Father's eyes tells me he understands.

Then I realize I have no idea how he got rid of that woman and made it over to me without her mercilessly killing us all. I glance around searching for any sign of her. It doesn't take me long to find her though. She's lying on the ground by where Father was restraining her, blood pooling around her. If I hadn't been frozen in pain right now, I'd be frozen in shock. The stake I pictured flying through the air and piercing her chest is sticking out of the middle of her sternum.

Father scans around us and yells, "Raven!"

Then in the next instant, his face is back next to mine.

"Hang on, pumpkin we're gonna get you out of here." He glances back up in the direction I left Oak and Raven and calmly whistles this time, before yelling to Raven again. I don't know how he is staying so calm through all of this, but I am extremely thankful for it.

I look back at the woman, wondering if she's dead, but as I stare, I can see her chest slowly rising and falling. I realize if she can live through a stake to the chest then we have no chance against her. With that thought, another wave of pain wracks my body causing my back to arch uncontrollably. It feels like my back is going to break. Through the haze of pain, I am faintly aware of hooves carefully walking up next to my head. Then there is a sensation of me being lifted off the ground and placed gently in Raven's saddle with my head resting on her neck. I think I'm left alone, but then from somewhere far off I hear my Father's soft calming voice.

"Pumpkin, we're getting you out of here. Raven will take care of you. Always remember I love you more than anything and you are the future of our people. Take your rightful place on the throne. Goodbye for now." I feel him gently kiss me on the forehead.

I struggle to say something, anything. I want to argue and tell him I don't want to leave without him. He needs to leave with me, but another wave of pain wracks my body causing all the muscles in my back to spasm. I scream through the pain, but it doesn't help alleviate any of the torturous agony, I feel like I am being crushed in a vise and no matter how much I scream it's not enough.

The smoke is thickening, and the world is still shaking. Everything vibrates as I search for camp, I can't see it anymore. I turn my head, as much as I can with the awkward way I'm laying on the saddle. I search where Oak should be laying, but I can't see him. All I see is Father whispering something to Raven. Then he pets her one last time on the forehead and Raven takes off.

I try to yell out *No! Dad!* but the pain wracking my body cuts off any words I try to form and turns them into a yell of agony. Behind us I can hear the woman screaming again, and see my father running away from us towards camp. He runs through the smoke, his figure turns hazy, almost ghostlike, getting cloudier and murkier until I can no longer see a figure at all, only the wisp of his outline moving in the distance.

The pain is getting to be too much. I am starting to feel lightheaded and woozy, then there's sensation like I'm hovering above myself, like my consciousness is outside of my body. Out of nowhere a huge, beautiful crack arcs across the sky. It's the white of pure power, like a thunderbolt forged by the God of thunder and lightning himself. As it lands right in the middle of camp, the following explosion is ethereal and world shattering.

By now Raven's ungodly speed has gotten us far enough away to not be touched by the ensuing fireball of fury, but my skin feels hot. I can feel the heat of the explosion on my face. I vaguely hear myself cry out for Father before I succumb to the excruciating pain and everything goes dark.

17

ALLISTER

WALKING INTO THE KING'S OMINOUSLY DARK THRONE ROOM, the first thing that catches my eye are the guards. Two Fae guards flank the door leading in, and two more flank the colossal dais before me.

The guards are swathed from head to toe in golden armor. Their heads are adorned with full-faced helmets with long golden feathers poking out the top of them. Golden scale armor runs down the length of their bodies; even their boots are fully protected in the same gold armor. Fae families in our kingdom are starving, and here the king is sitting on his throne, protected by guards whose armor alone could feed fifty families for a year. It's disgusting. These guards are the king's golden guards, his protection unit, the best of the best—except for myself, of course.

I am strictly the king's personal slayer, the kingdom's greatest warrior, trusted with dispatching of the most sensitive targets. Henrik, King of the Western Fae sits on a huge black throne. The throne itself is forged out of charred bones of the humans Henrik killed over the years. Atop a smaller but matching throne next to him sits Kenda, my mother, and Queen of the Eastern Fae. Which, through marriage, makes Henrik the King of all Fae.

Now, as I walk into the throne room, the first, most menacing thing I see is Henrik. Henrik is a big, bulky man; not fat, but muscular. His gray beard reaches from his aquiline nose down to his broad chest. His hair is short, salt and pepper colored, and his piercing eyes are the color of fresh blood. He may have become my stepfather when I was young, but I didn't delude myself, I know exactly where I stand with him, a competitor for the throne. He puts up with me for now because of my slaying skills, but that won't last forever.

I cross the immense, dark, marble floor to stand in front of them. As I peer up at the king and queen, I see they are both clad in matching golden tunics. The tunic overwhelms my mother. The two of them are polar opposites, where the King is big and muscular my mother is dainty and feminine. The clothing almost makes Henrik seem commendable, but I know that is not the case. Henrik is the scariest man I have ever seen in my life. It isn't necessarily his appearance, which scares me, although his features are terrifying, it's what I know he is capable of.

Henrik is hundreds of years old and inherited his throne from his father at the young age of 221. Inherited probably isn't the right word for it. Overtook is a better word for what happened. Henrik's father was poisoned during a dinner party with a rival tribe. The chief of that tribe, my father, was blamed and executed.

Henrik became king overnight and overtook the rival tribe by forcing my mother to be his bride, gaining more people and land under his rule. Some said Henrik had poisoned his own father, killing two birds with one stone. But the people who said such things usually didn't live terribly long. I think back to that night all those years ago, to the truth.

I was only five years old when all this happened. Too young for anyone to take seriously but by chance I know, firsthand, what happened all those years ago. So does my mother, but she was, and is, too frightened of Henrik to speak out against him and I don't blame her.

During that fateful stay at the palace, all those years ago I was mostly ignored, so I spent my days exploring the palace. I remember I was playing spy and sneaking down each and every corridor I could find without being spotted.

Soon enough, I was in the belly of the palace, lost. I turned a corner and walked right into Titania, the king's only daughter. She peered straight down at me and at the same instant I heard the king yell her name from behind her.

Before turning to Henrik, Titania whispered down to me, "Run."

I was frozen in place, scared out of my mind as Titania turned around to face her father. As she turned around, she smoothly pushed me back down the hallway I had just sneaked down, which was exactly what I needed to pull me out of my reverie. I turned and ran back the way I came, back around a corner, but instead of running away, I did what a real spy would do and hid behind a statue, listening.

From my vantage point, I could hear everything being said between Titania and Henrik.

"Is everything ready for tonight?"

"Yes, father."

"Where is the poison?"

"In the hands of a trusted individual. It will be done before dessert."

"I hope you're right, because if this thing does not go off without a hitch it will be you who I hang."

"Yes, sir," she tightly voiced, ending their exchange.

After hearing their exchange, I turned heel and ran away. I found my way back to my mother's room and told her everything I heard. Of course, she didn't believe me. She thought it was all just part of the spy game I was playing, which made me think these crazy things. I insisted that wasn't the case so emphatically she quickly got tired of arguing with me and sent me to my room to have supper instead of with the other royals. Now thinking back, I'm sure she was worried I would say something and cause trouble for our kingdom.

So the adults had dinner without me. I ate dinner alone and crawled into bed for the night hoping mother was right and everything I heard was just a figment of my imagination, but I knew in my heart it wasn't.

Afterwards, right as I was falling off to sleep, my mother quietly stepped into my room. She glided over to my bed, sat down, and kissed me on the forehead. Then as she got up to leave, she whispered, "I'm sorry." The next day, I would find out Henrik was now blaming my father for poisoning and killing his father.

My mother came to me later that morning and we agreed not to ever talk about what I overheard the previous day ever again for the sake of our people back home. She also told me Henrik had informed her for this slight against his household he would start a war with our nation unless she married him. She explained she would do this to keep bloodshed from reaching our border. But we later found out in exchange for peace she would never be the same woman again.

She gave up her freedom for our people, for me, but now

she sits on a throne by her second husband whom she knows murdered the love of her life. She sits there like a statue; unmoving and uncaring of what happens around her. I don't know if she even realizes who I am as I walk through the throne room toward her and Henrik.

Henrik has called for me many times over the years but not like this. Today, while training with my squad, one of Henrik's golden guards came to tell me I was being summoned under gag order to drop whatever I was doing and head to the throne room immediately.

As the leader of Henrik's top death squad, I hadn't ever been so accosted especially with a gag order. My squad has never once been exempted on mission details. There is nothing in this world my men can't handle, so why would Henrik need to be so secretive? Why call for me only?

I kneel down at the bottom of the steps to the throne with my head bowed and a fisted hand over my heart in a show of allegiance.

"You may stand." Henrik's booming voice fills the room.

I rise and place my hands behind my back staring into those bloodthirsty eyes.

"What can I do for you, my liege?" I ask in my most humble voice.

"I need you to fulfill a mission for me."

"Me and my squad would be honored." I bow.

"No, only you this time Allister. Not your squad. This is a top secret mission for you and you, alone."

"Yes, of course, sire," spills out, but I have a million questions coursing through my mind. Why only me? What is so secretive I have to do this alone? But before I can finish my thoughts Henrik continues.

"I'm sure you felt the quake of an Awakening the other day."

"Yes sire, one of our Fae must have gone through their Awakening. I didn't think much of it."

"None of *our* Fae Awakened. That was an outsider."

This shocks me. "But we felt the quake here, how is such a thing possible?"

"I've known about this particular Fae girl for some years. She's of mixed blood. How she's survived for this long, I don't know. I knew she was close to her Awakening so I sent a werewolf out to dispatch her, but it didn't return. I don't know how she overcame the werewolf, but she did. When the werewolf didn't return, I sent out one of my special projects and that's when she Awakened, and my special project was also lost. So, as you can see, we have a problem on our hands. She's a rogue Fae, and she could be the most powerful Fae of this generation even though she's only a disgusting half breed." He glares at me with his cold dead eyes, his emotions, like usual, unreadable.

"So, you want me to capture her and turn her to our side so we can use her power?" I question.

Henrik sends me a seething stare and screams "No! I want it dead! It's past the point of being one of us. It needs to be put down."

I don't think before I blurt out, "But why?"

Henrik explodes. Fire encompasses his body. I drop to a knee again and a torrent of fire shoots past where my head had just been seconds ago as Henrik bellows, "You do not get to ask me why I make my decisions. I am your king, and you will do this for me without question."

I put my fisted hand back over my heart and bow my head as low as possible as I say, "Yes sire, of course," in my most non-threatening voice.

"My adviser will give you the information regarding where she was last seen and you can go from there." I stand up and turn to leave, but at my back Henrik yells, "If you disappoint me boy don't even bother coming back." I spin back around to face him and bow my head to my king.

I knew something was up from the moment Henrik summoned me, but I didn't realize how serious the situation was until now. I am his top slayer, the leader of his top death squad. If he's willing to kill me for failing to kill a little girl, there must be something else different about this half Fae. There must be something extraordinary about her.

With my head still bowed in submission, I back out of the room without turning my back on Henrik again. I want him to continue thinking I am on his side. As I walk through the castle, I have a million thoughts cascading through my mind, all of them about this half Fae girl.

18

ATTINA

I WAKE UP TO THE BRIGHT LIGHT OF A NEW DAY AND THE swaying movement of Raven under me. The sun is already high in the sky by the time I open my heavy eyes.

Every single inch of my body aches and my skin feels too warm from lying in the sun all day on Raven's back. My lips are dry and tough, and I can feel my lips have cracked and are peeling away. My throat is so arid it feels like I swallowed a mouthful of sand and my sweat ridden clothes are clinging to my skin like I've had a fever all night and it finally broke.

I try to clear my throat, but can't. It feels like I have rocks stuck in there. "Raven I'm up. Stop for a minute," I croak out. I don't know how long I've been asleep, but with the way my throat aches, it must have been a long time.

Raven abruptly stops and I try to keep my balance, but I'm too weak and I sail over her shoulder landing hard on the ground on my back. After moving on horseback for so long I simply lay there taking in the feeling of stillness. Raven moves so her head is directly above mine blocking out the sun and I can feel her warm breath graze my face.

"You okay, kid?"

Hearing her voice hits me like a ton of bricks and I instantly start crying uncontrollably but through the fog of tears I hear Raven's voice, shrill and concerned as she says, "What's wrong? Are you hurt? What's going on?"

I take a deep breath and slowly let it out before I sit up and turn to Raven to answer her. "I'm just so overwhelmed. What happened? Where's Father? Where's Oak?" I say, searching around us, finding nothing. Raven drops her head and stares down at the ground before answering and I know that can't mean anything good.

"What do you remember after your Awakening took hold?"

I think back. My memory is extremely hazy and they are clouded with pain, but there are a few things, which actually stand out.

"I remember falling on the ground and the massive pain wracking my body. Father was restraining that woman. I kept thinking about that huge splinter of wood driving straight through her heart, then a feeling of relief. Somehow after that, Father was by my side and I saw that woman bleeding out hurt on the ground. Then he picked me up, put me on your back, and after that all I remember is the unending pain. I saw Father walk back to camp and I tried to yell out to him but all I could do was scream and then I remember a blinding white light."

Raven kneels down on all fours so she is on the ground face to face with me. She takes in a deep steadying breath and begins. "Attina, first off you must know that woman at camp was your mother. I don't know if Silas ever told you her name, but her name is Titania."

My jaw drops. I try to say something, but all that falls out of my mouth is a croaking noise. I remember now, Oak screamed at Raven that Titania was there. I didn't realize it at the time, but that was what Father said my mother's name was.

"Second, her power was weather manipulation. I don't know if you noticed with everything going on, but by the time we made it back to camp together there was a dark ominous cloud cover circling the camp. That white light you saw while we were leaving was lightning striking the ground. We barely made it out of the strike zone. I don't know how anyone could have survived that kind of explosion. I'm so sorry, but we must continue on without them, we must accept that they are gone my lady," she says this last part with a sadness in her voice and a bow of her head.

"No!" I shout, scrambling to my feet, my mind moving faster than my body's capabilities. My legs are so weak I fall back down and sit, dazed. I whisper, "They can't be gone... they can't be gone."

I vaguely realize Raven is saying something to me, but I'm too far away in my own world to hear her. I'm flipping through my memories of Father and Oak. Each and every laugh, smile, hug, and support they gave me over the years. How Oak and Father always protected me above everything else. They can't be gone. I still need protecting. I wrap my arms around myself while rocking back and forth. I feel like a child trying to soothe themselves, but it's the only thing that helps.

As I sit on the ground rocking myself, I see wind blowing around my body, encircling me. I search around, nowhere else is the wind blasting, only around me. Then I notice water seeping up from the desert floor and pebbles around me start shaking. This must be my Fae powers, how am I supposed to do this? Mother said Father and Oak would help me with this part but now they're gone.

Seeing my powers taking over on their own makes me think how helpless I undoubtedly am now. Father and Oak would know what to do. I won't ever be able to control my powers without them. I can feel myself fracturing on the inside and somehow, I can physically hear the cracks spreading through me. How am I supposed to do this on my own? It's impossible.

Raven's voice breaks through to me, through the splinters, and smashing the haze covering my mind. I gape, and see her shouting at me, but can barely hear what she's saying over the sound of the wind circling me. I strain my ears and her words drift to me as a whisper

"Calm down! Breathe Attina! You're going to hurt yourself."

I start to breathe deeply, in and out, and as I do the winds calm some.

"Attina, breathe damnit!" Now I can hear it for the shout it is.

I continue slowly and breathing deeply, over and over, in and out.

Then out of nowhere everything stops. The wind is still. The rocks around me have all moved away and now I sit in a crevice; like the earth around me tried to block me from the world, like it tried to wrap me in a protective bubble. I continue to rhythmically breathe, each breath calming me more and more. Then Raven's face is right next to mine.

"Are you okay, Attina?"

I breathe in again. "Yes, I think so."

Raven explodes. "You scared me! What the hell just happened?"

"I don't know. I guess those were my Fae powers coming out," I say meekly.

"You better tell me what's going on right now!" I can tell

by the expression on her face she's annoyed, it's the same expression she had anytime she had to deal with me growing up.

"I don't know!" I yell. "I was thinking about Father and Oak being gone and I wrapped my arms around myself and thought how comforting it was and the winds started. Then I thought about how I'd never be able to control my powers without them and things just got worse from there..." I trail off.

Raven glares at me. "Well you could've got both of us killed, and then what would their deaths have been for? To save you just so you could kill yourself with your own stupidity?"

Her voice softens. "They died protecting you. Do you hear me? They both died protecting us. Protecting you. Neither of them could've asked for a better, more honorable death."

"They could have died of old age," I say utterly defeated.

Raven drops her head. "Yes, they could have, but they wouldn't be able to live a life without you in it, my lady, and that's what would've happened. Titania would have killed you, and they would've been left without you. No, this is the death they would have wanted."

My shoulders shake while sobs wrack through my body uncontrollably. I start to fold into myself again. Apparently, it infuriates Raven because she jumps up on all four hooves with her head hanging down a hair's width away from my face.

"I will not let you sully their deaths by falling apart on me and almost killing yourself again. They died protecting what they loved and believed in. Their deaths were honorable, a warrior's death. You do not get to be a spoiled brat and make this about you." Raven violently pushes me over onto my back with her head and turns and walks away.

Her outburst is such a shock. All I can do is lay there staring up at the sun, thinking. Trying to calm myself by taking deep steadying breaths. It takes a couple of minutes, but my breathing starts to normalize again, and the tears slow down.

The gears in my brain start working again and my thoughts become clearer. Maybe Raven is right. I'm definitely no warrior, but the three of them are—or were—so she would know their outlook on life and death better than I ever could. I know I was the most important thing to both of them. Neither of them would want to see me falling apart like this and losing control of my powers or myself. They risked their lives without a second thought at every turn. Just then it hits me, and I sit up. "I'm an orphan now."

Raven lifts her head from the lone patch of grass she's eating and glances at me with soft eyes. "So am I, but we have each other, and we have a mission we need to fulfill, or their deaths will have been for nothing..." she bows her head before finishing with, "my lady." These last words give me strength and solidify my resolve. I nod my head to Raven, then stand, my sword reassuringly bumps against my side as I move.

"How long have I been out?"

"Two and a half days."

I lose my balance and sidestep "What?"

"Yeah, I was starting to get worried. If you didn't wake up soon, I was thinking I'd have to buck you off and send you flying," she says with an ornery wink.

I stick my tongue out at her like the adult I am. For a split second everything seems like it will be okay, but my heavy heart knows that's not true. Nothing will ever be okay or the same again.

"So, what's the plan, Raven?"

She moves closer to me, her sleek body glistening in the afternoon sun. I always forget how athletic she is until times like now where the sun is shining perfectly off her muscular body. "Well, I thought we would stick to the original plan and head to Sanctuary. I'm sure you're missing James."

The color rises in my cheeks and I stare at the ground to try and hide it. I do miss him. More than I want to admit, and who knows what he will think of me. We take off without a word. I mean I didn't know we were leaving when we did, but he could still be mad. I wonder what everyone told him to get him to leave without me.

"Okay, sounds like a great plan to me. Where are we anyway?"

"Well, I've been walking pretty much nonstop since we left camp. I don't know what supplies we have in the saddle bags but I got us to the outskirts of Hugyo. We should be able to find some supplies there."

I stand up happily surprised my legs support my own weight already. "Let's go." I say as I start walking past Raven. She's carried me enough, it's time for me to walk on my own and give her a break. I take a few steps before being recalled by Raven.

"Hey, wait, kid!" she says trotting up to my side. I notice my bow and arrows somehow made it out of camp with us and the thought of still having something so precious with me makes me smile. "We need to be smart about this. It's only you and me now, there's no back up coming this time around. I need you to trust me a little and take my lead on this."

As I think about it, I walk over to Raven and pull my bow

and arrows off of her back and strap it to my own. Can I trust Raven after her cruelness all these years? A few days ago, I would've said no to her question but we've been through so much together in a short amount of time and I realize I do trust her, completely.

"Of course, Raven, I trust you."

She stares at me with her warm gray eyes, and I can tell she took my statement to heart and it's comforting for me to see her happy. Even through all this, losing my father, losing her father, she's still somehow able to smile.

Raven stands there staring at me with something like love filling her eyes until I say, "What do you want to do?" This pulls her out of her reverie, and she blinks then turns her head towards the city ahead.

"We need to scout this out. See if there are people still living in this town, try to determine if they're friendly, but most of all we need to check for multiple exits. I don't want any surprises, but if we do run into trouble, I want us to know a few ways out." I nod and we head into Hugyo.

The town of Hugyo is located down in a desert valley. The top of the valley is filled with thick, luscious, verdant trees like back home, but now we're hitting another kind of land-scape, heat and desert.

We round the valley on the south side of town, keeping close to the last of the tree line. When we get parallel to the town it's easy to see it's abandoned. I glance over to Raven. "Okay, I want you to skirt the town on this side to the end of town. I'll meet you at the end of town when I get our supplies. Try to keep an eye out for me, but if you lose sight of me for more than ten minutes you can search for me. Sound good?"

Raven stares at me with awe and conviction. She bows her head and says, "You're turning into an awfully smart warrior. But kid, if you think I'm leaving you after that breakdown and insane show of power—you're crazy." She smiles at me then winks before walking off towards the edge of town. I walk down the hill and head for town glancing around for any sign of life.

We walk around the perimeter of the entire town, staying hidden in case of enemy eyes. We note a few exits out of town in different directions and as soon as we make it back to our starting spot, we head down the main road through Hugyo. As we walk, Raven does give me a little room to be on my own and stays to the outside edge of town, which I appreciate, but catching glimpses of her as I pass between buildings is off putting because I keep jumping at her outline.

As we get to the heart of the town, I can finally see the state of things. It seems like everyone merely picked up and left one day. Doors are left wide open, and I can see the stores still have merchandise in them. I walk by what I assume is the town bar—we didn't have one in Daruk, but I read about them in some of Father's books growing up—and there is still food left on the tables. From outside, I can smell the pungent odor of rotting food. Drawn by the smell, flies fill the building, making the structure almost vibrate from the buzzing.

I move away from the stench and migrate into the middle of the main road and take a glimpse around at my surroundings. The town is only a little bit bigger than my hometown. I turn behind me to the start of town and in my peripheral. I see a shadow at the edge of town by the tree line. I turn my head as fast as I can, but by the time I turn around completely the shadow is gone. Did I actually see someone, or were my eyes playing tricks on me again?

It couldn't have been Raven, she would have had to get around the entire town and there hasn't been enough time. Maybe someone stayed in the town by themselves? I stare at the tree line a little longer, straining my eyes to find the shadow again. I see nothing but the unmoving, blank tree line. I glance to where I think Raven will be to ask her if she saw the same shadow I did, but she's nowhere to be found now.

"Raven?" I call out questioningly.

"Yes? You okay, kid?" She sounds like she must be standing behind one of the houses which line the main street, so I was right, what I saw couldn't have been her.

"I'm fine. I was just wondering where you were." I was right, that shadow wasn't her. I wonder what it was then.

As I continue my journey, I see the town market and walk in. I know we need food and water at the very least. As I walk inside, I am again hit by the stench of rot. I plug my nose and force my feet to move. Everything that used to be fresh in the market is now rotten, so I'll have to stick to preserved food and rice.

I walk down the few isles in the store picking up jars of dried meat. There aren't many jars left, so I clean out the store. As I walk to the back of the store, I notice a satchel and grab it, shoving the jars inside as I walk. The next isle has rice in it and I grab a few bags filling the rest of the pack. At the end of the rice isle there are even pots to cook in. I grab a medium sized one and strap it to a clasp on the bag.

By now I'm used to the awful smell and no longer have to plug my nose, but I also can't wait to get away from all these flies incessantly landing on me. I take the satchel and strap it on. I won't be able to use my bow like this but it's the easiest way to carry everything and I still have my sword strapped to my thigh. I run to the door of the market and as I do, I notice by the door is a big water display. The water is held in small kegs with leather handles to carry them with. I pick up one keg in each hand and head out the door. My lucky day!

Being back outside in the sunshine without such an awful smell permeating my skin is refreshing. I'm proud of myself. I did a good job. We'll have food, water, and a pot to cook in and when the water runs out, we'll have a pot to boil dirty water in to make it drinkable... we can do this, we can make it to Sanctuary. I know we can.

I walk out of town without incident and meet Raven right on the outskirts, just like we planned. I strap the satchel and kegs to her saddle, climb back in the saddle, and we're back on the road to Sanctuary.

19

ALLISTER

From high in the treetops, I lay in wait.

Henrik sent me here to kill the girl who caused the colossal Awakening quake, but I'm still not sure why. Why is the king so scared of this little girl? I need to know before I kill her. He told me he'd already unleashed a werewolf and some crazed Fae he created on her, and yet this little girl is still somehow alive. How is such a thing possible?

Even from far away I can tell she isn't one hundred percent Fae. She walks clumsily like a human, but is slightly quicker than a human would be. She has the lithe figure of a Fae, but her ears are so slightly pointed it's hard to tell if they look Fae or not. She travels with a Fae horse too, where could she have gotten such an animal? At first, I was worried she might be traveling with a Fae, which could make killing her harder, but I've been stalking them for a few days and I haven't seen anyone else with them.

I meant to take her down as soon as she got away from that Fae horse, but as she was walking towards town, I saw her face and something changed in me. Her beautiful eyes sparkled, and something behind them held me captive. A knot formed in my chest, which hadn't been there before. I'd heard stories of this kind of feeling before, but this is the first time I've felt it for myself.

There is something about this girl. I can feel it in my bones.

She is obviously awkward walking with a beautiful Fae sword trapped around her hips. I can tell by the way she overcompensates for the weight she isn't used to it. The bow is a different story though. Even with it only strapped to her back, I can tell it's a part of her. The way she moves to stay out of the bows way while she walks tells me she uses it daily. I bet she could easily hit me from here if she wanted to.

So, it surprises the hell out of me when she walks out of one of the buildings with a pack covering her back and covering her bow, rookie mistake. She would be helpless if she were to be attacked by anything, sword or no sword.

I watch her for a little while longer. I need to know what is so incredibly special about this girl, and how I can use it to my advantage.

20

ATTINA

Raven and I ride through the rest of the day, there is only a few hours of light left after we leave town, and Raven is exhausted, so on our way we find a small cliff to make camp under. I climb down out of the saddle and start to unsaddle Raven.

"We haven't passed many trees or woods, so we won't be able to make a fire tonight, Attina."

"Well, it looks like we'll have to get close tonight to keep warm," I say winking at her, trying to lighten the mood.

"But seriously, you've gone above and beyond these past few days. We're traveling into the desert so it's only going to get hotter the closer we get to Sanctuary, so I want us to start traveling at night. Tonight, and tomorrow, I want you to rest and we can start again tomorrow night. You deserve it after dragging me around unconscious for two days. Does that sound good to you?"

By now, I've pulled off Raven's saddle and we both climb under the cliff to lay down. She glances up at me with her heavy sleepy eyes. "Okay, we can do that." Then her eyes drift down to my sword. "But I want you practicing with your sword every chance you get. Deal?"

"Deal." Raven drops her head and falls fast asleep. I drag the saddle, saddle pad, and our bags under the cliff with us and crawl next to Raven. I lay with my body curled up between her legs and my head resting on her front leg. It surprises me how much I trust her after such a little time. My whole life we've butted heads, and now here I am cuddled between her legs trusting her completely. Even her presence and warmth is so comforting I fall fast into a deep sleep.

Over the next few days we fall into a routine. We travel at night and right as the sun is coming up over the horizon we find somewhere to rest for the day. Sometimes finding a cliff and sometimes we have to dig our own little cave and cover ourselves with the saddle pad for some shade. The pad smells of horse sweat and is heavy from use but it is a lot better than getting burned by the sun.

Each night before bed, I practice my sword skills. Raven usually watches and is surprisingly good at teaching me how to strike and move properly. After a few days of her teaching, I can already see a huge difference in my performance.

I'm less wary of holding the deadly weapon, it's more comfortable in my hands, and I'm not so worried about accidentally cutting off an appendage anymore. The more I practice, the lighter the sword gets in my hands and each movement with it becomes smoother. I feel like I'm becoming a real swords-woman.

We have been rationing our water our whole trip but for the last day we've been out of water and since we're in the desert, we haven't found any natural springs either. The next town can't appear soon enough. We're both so dehydrated,

I'm slumped in the saddle and Raven's feet are dragging as her head hangs low to the ground not wanting to expend the energy to keep her head up. So, when I finally see Salhay on the horizon, it gives me some hope.

"Raven, we don't have the luxury of scoping this place out beforehand. We both desperately need water now. We're going to head into that town and we'll just have to watch each other's backs."

Raven picks up her head and pricks her ears. "I don't think that's a very wise plan. Too many things could go wrong."

Then Raven trips over her own two feet almost falling down to her chest. I dismount and jerk her by the bridle so her face is right next to my face.

"We're both dangerously dehydrated. You can barely keep your own feet underneath you. We are both going into that town, we're going to find water, and we are going to rehydrate before we leave town." I command.

Raven lets her head hang, this time defeated. "Yes, my lady."

Both of us are quiet the rest of the way to Salhay, keeping our guard up for anything out of the ordinary. We both search our surroundings and the horizon for some sign of danger but again this town is abandoned. I swear I see something on the edge of my periphery, but each time I swing my head around to get a better view of it, there isn't anything there.

We make it to town without incident, and quickly find the market. Salhay isn't much of a town, only a market and houses. Like the last town this market is inundated with flies, but this time instead of a normal rot smell the air almost feels sweetly sticky. Raven takes one step inside the market before she starts coughing uncontrollably and she turns right around and walks back outside. I follow her out.

"My nose is too sensitive, and the stench is too much for me. I'll wait outside while you grab supplies. Yell if you need me, I'll be able to hear you from here."

"Okay, just keep watch out here." I say as I unstrap the pack from her saddle. I throw the pack over my shoulder, covering my bow again. I wander inside, my thoughts drifting to the outside world. What is this incessant feeling I keep getting of being watched? In the back of my mind, I hear a small rustling sound. I stop and scan around but don't see anything. I think to myself *it must be rats fattening up on all this wasted food.*

My thoughts turn back to that ever-growing feeling of being watched I've had these past few days. Even since walking into this market the feeling has gotten worse. Should I tell Raven? It might unduly worry her, but what if it really is something? My Fae powers should be coming to me by now after my Awakening, maybe I have a heightened sense of awareness too?

Then *bam!*

I'm pulled out of my reverie by something big slamming into my back and before I realize it I'm on my back, pinned down. The pack covers my head and neck as I slam hard against the tiled ground. Claws dig into the backs of my arms, holding me down. In shock, I scream out a shrill gurgling scream.

I try to pull away, scratching and clawing at anything to get away from whatever is holding me down but in the next instant I hear hooves. Then the creature's claws rip from my arms and the weight of it rolls over my head and away from me. I reel away from the creature and roll backwards into Raven's legs. Raven puts her head down protectively and snorts. I maneuver my head around hers to take in what attacked me and realize it's a Solis.

This one is a woman. Patches of her hair have been ripped right out of her scalp. Her nails are exaggeratedly long like a predator's claws, the color of dirt, and they have my blood dripping off of their sharp tips. Her clothes are non-existent and the skin covering her skeletal naked body is scale-like. The stench permeating from her is what smelled so sweetly rotten in this building. I can't believe I didn't smell her when she stalked up behind me before she attacked me.

I turn, grab on to Raven's leg, and pull myself up on wobbly legs. The Solis just stands there watching in a crouched position growling, looking like a wild starved animal, not sure if she wants to take us both on alone. I hear Raven behind me.

"You need to finish this. Dispose of this creature. Put her out of her misery."

I'm still in a daze from being knocked to the ground so roughly all I can do is nod.

Without thinking I start pulling the pack off of my shoulder to get to my bow but as soon as I touch the bag, I hear Raven behind me.

"Not with the bow. Use the sword, you need to know what killing with it feels like."

I nod silently again. She's right. This needs to be done. I can do this. I take a deep breath and reach to my hip. I hear a loud growl and the Solis starts running at me with her claws out like she knows I want to kill her, and she's going to try and scratch my eyes out for it.

I get my sword pulled out and pointed at the Solis before I freeze with fear. I've killed many animals over the years but never a human, or I guess something that used to be human.

I hold my sword out toward the Solis, and it impales itself on the end of my sword, running it's full body to the hilt, it's dried out dirty body squelching down the edges of my blade, before slumping down.

I drop my sword in shock and back away from the corpse right into Raven's chest. Milliseconds before I feel the woman's scaled hand grab my ankle, Raven yells in my ear, "She's not dead until you cut off the head." I glance down at the Solis as it's gaping maw reaches for my calf.

I wrench my leg away, but she's digging in deep with her claws. I slice down with all my strength and cut through the Solis's neck like a knife slicing through water. The body of the Solis finally slides against the ground and doesn't move again.

Without saying a word, I wipe the blade off on the woman's back and resheathe it. I squat down and start to pry the Solis's hand off of my ankle. Blood trickles down my ankle and both of my arms.

Quietly, I stand. Without thinking, I walk off away from Raven and away from the dead Solis. I faintly hear Raven saying something, but my mind is coated with dense fog. I walk down a different isle with no real direction, in a daze, until Raven pushes me from behind. I fall flat on my knees and the palms of my hands, bringing me out of the haze and I hear Raven.

"Holy crap kid, are you okay?" I nod. "I was calling you and calling you and you had this blank expression on your face and kept walking away from me. I had to nudge you to get you to respond to me."

All of a sudden, I have tears pouring down my face. "Raven" I choke out. "I just killed a person, a real person. How could I do such a thing? How can I live with myself?" I start drowning in my tears. My mind starts running and the muscles in my back are ravaged from the vivacity of the sobs escaping my lungs.

Raven nudges me. "Hey kid, it's okay. You had to kill her. She was attacking you. You had to fight for your life. Besides, she was a Solis, you did her a favor by giving her the true death. Now she can rest in peace."

"She was a *person!*" I shout, as I turn away and walk off.

Raven doesn't follow me. After taking a few breaths I realize I'm not sure why I yelled at Raven. I know she's right, but in that moment I needed to scream.

I wipe my tears and walk around the market filling our pack back up with supplies and grab two more kegs of water before heading to the front door. Raven is waiting there, but I can't meet her gaze just yet.

I stride outside with the supplies and hear Raven following me. Without turning around I yell back to her "We're going to stay in one of the houses here. We're both too dehydrated to continue, it will be light soon and I don't feel like walking through the heat. According to the map, the next town is only around a day away so we will be there by this time tomorrow." Raven says nothing back but I hear her continue following me as I head for the closest house.

It's not much to gander at. The house, like the rest of the buildings in town, is made out of clay bricks with a wooden front door. There are two windows facing the main road, one on each side of the wooden door. Sheets hang on the inside of the building covering the windows.

I unsheathe my sword again and kick open the door. It slams and smashes back against the front wall. I walk in. Thankful this house has only one room. The room is sparse. The only thing in it is a couch, a bed, and a small toilet and basin in the corner. I check under the couch and under the bed but this house is empty, just like the rest of this town. I turn around as Raven's hulking structure squeezes through the door, then I step out behind her closing and locking the door. The air feels thick with words unsaid.

"Look Raven, I'm sorry—" I start as I turn to face her, but she cuts me off.

"Kid, it's fine, I get it. This is a tougher world than you ever knew and getting used to that fact comes with growing pains. If I were in your shoes, I would have probably yelled at me too. No hard feelings."

Her response shocks me. Seriously? No hard feelings? No shitty comment? No making me grovel? I know we have a different relationship now, but I figured she'd give me some hell for how I behaved. "You sure?" I ask skeptically.

Raven bows her head and smiles from her eyes as she says, "Yes my lady, I am sure."

I walk over to her and wrap my arms around her neck and snuggle my face into her shoulder. "Thank you, Raven."

"You've been through a lot, let's get you to bed."

I nod my head and move to her side and start unsaddling her, as I work my mind calms. Then I grab the pack and pour some water out into our pot for Raven to drink.

"Are you hungry? There's no hay or grass in town but I can cook you something" I ask Raven.

After she finishes drinking, she lifts her head and says, "Just tired. Let's get some sleep, we can eat tomorrow." Raven somehow fits herself on the couch putting her head between her legs on the arm of it and falls deep asleep.

I finish the other keg of water and clean my wounds before crawling into bed. The sheets have a smell of old dust and dirt to them, and they have a rough almost gritty texture, but sleeping in a bed is so much nicer than sleeping on the cold hard ground.

Before I try to fall asleep, I reach next to the bed and

search in my quiver, pulling out the family picture I took from my childhood home. Tears fill my eyes. Now they're both gone. I would give anything to be able to talk to them one more time. I wrap my arms around the small frame, and it doesn't take long before my exhausted body relaxes and I quickly fall into a deep fitful sleep with our picture still clutched to my chest.

21

ATTINA

I WAKE BY AFTERNOON THE NEXT DAY, RAVEN IS STILL SLEEPING on the couch so I slip out of the house with my bow and quiver strapped to my back and my sword hanging low on my hip. For the next couple of hours I practice. I shoot arrows into the building across the street and practice unsheathing and re-sheathing my sword over and over again until it is second nature, until I can do it without thinking. This is no small feat. I fight mercilessly with the shadows until the sun is threatening to set. I've practiced everyday on our long journey, and my progress is showing. The sword feels lighter, and I feel like it's beginning to be a part of me, like my bow is.

Sheathing my sword and collecting my arrows, I head back to the town market, only walking inside so far as to grab us two more kegs of water for our journey. I do not want to set eyes on the Solis woman lying there dead because of me.

When I walk back through the front door of the house, Raven is finally starting to stir. She must have slept well because she seems confused and disheveled when she sees me in the door.

"Good morning sleepy head. I let you sleep for as long as I could, but we need to eat and get back on the road, the sun is starting to set."

"Are you sweating?" she asks, confused.

"I've been outside practicing the past couple of hours." Raven smiles and I smile back continuing, "Come on, let's get on the road." After a quick meal, I get Raven resaddled and we head out of town.

The feeling of being watched is getting stronger and stronger as the night drags on. It's getting to the point where I can't ignore the problem any longer. I keep spinning around in the saddle searching all around us.

"Kid, what's the matter? Why are you so squirrely up there?"

I answer her, but keep my eyes peeled around us. "Do you feel like we're being watched?"

"I haven't really caught on to anyone following us, but with your Fae powers blossoming I would listen to your gut feeling on this. What do you want to do about it?"

"I'm not sure, but we're going to have to do something about it by the time we make it to Fedum."

We sit in silence for the next few hours, contemplating what to do when we get to the next town. If there is someone following us, we have to handle it here. It's the last town before Sanctuary, and there is no way we can allow anyone to follow us there to our townspeople.

"Okay Raven, I can only think of one plan. It's a long shot and you're not gonna like it, so if you have any other ideas now is the time to speak up."

Raven just shakes her head dejectedly.

"Well, if I'm right, whoever is out there hasn't shown

himself while we've been together. The only times I've caught glimpses of him or her were while I was alone. So, we need to split up."

At this Raven stops so abruptly it unseats me, and I almost fall off over the front of her shoulder. I wrap my arms around her neck to keep myself upright.

"No," is all she says with so much conviction and force in her voice, I second-guess arguing with her but I know there's no other way.

I softly say, "Raven," but she immediately interrupts me.

"No! I am the last one left to protect you. You're our future queen. This is too big of a risk. I won't allow it." I take a deep intake of air and let it out, thinking of everyone in Sanctuary, of James, and finally of Father and Oak.

"If I allow whoever or whatever this is to follow us to Sanctuary then Father and Oak's deaths will be for nothing. If whoever's following us is Fae, we will lead them right to Sanctuary, right to our townspeople, right to James."

"If you're killed, their deaths will have been for nothing!" Raven shouts.

I climb down off of Raven and walk to face her. I hold her sweet baby doll head between my hands and put my forehead on hers.

"Raven, I am to be queen. You will have to put some faith in me." Raven glances down to the beige, sizzling sand. I can tell she's sad and conflicted. "Those are my people at Sanctuary. I have to protect my people with everything in my being."

Raven lifts her head. "But you don't have to do it alone." I can hear her heart is no longer in the argument, she knows I'm right. She just doesn't like it.

I pat her head. "Yes, Raven, with this one I do need to do

it on my own. You will let me protect my people to my best ability or you will find another queen."

Shock registers on her face before Raven nods her head knowing she's lost the argument. "Okay, what's the plan, my lady?"

"It's simple. This is the last town before Sanctuary. The last chance we have to draw this person out before we lead them straight to all those innocent people. We're simply going to act like this is any other town. We scout it out, and then I head through town while you go around it. Then I'm going to hang out in this town by myself longer than usual. I have a feeling if I'm alone long enough this person will show themselves. If we're not being followed, then no problem, but if we are being followed, I will have to handle it. If I don't show up at the rendezvous point within an hour, then you better come find me." Raven glances at me with worried eyes. I smile at her. "Don't look so glum. Everything will be okay."

For the first time in my life, I give Raven a real hug, wrapping my arms around her neck. She leans into me and for a moment we just stand there in each other's arms. I breathe in her smell. She doesn't even smell like a horse to me anymore; she smells like home.

I'm the first one to pull away. "Let's get going and get this over with." I wink at her and turn to walk towards Fedum with Raven close behind me.

We do our usual walk through the town paying special attention to its Main Street, market, and houses. We eventually find multiple exits and escape routes, then agree on a place to meet up at the end of town. Raven drops me off at the start of town and heads off to our rendezvous point before I start my trek down through Fedum.

From the moment I split away from Raven, I feel the

ominous presence intensify. My body begins to pulse with an unknown sensation. I have a feeling I won't have to wait as long as I thought for whomever it is to show.

The further I get into town, the more intense the pulsation becomes, rolling through my body from my heart to my toes and back again. By the time I get into town, I feel like my body is not my own anymore. In my head I see images flashing by and I try to stay calm, but lately keeping a hold on my emotions has been tough. I tell myself over and over this is only my Fae side manifesting.

It takes a few minutes for me to figure out exactly what is happening and what I'm seeing, but I realize the flashes in my mind are from someone else's point of view, from a Fae's point of view, if I had to take a wild guess. I can see myself walking, my long brown hair swaying back and forth, my bow in my hand. The sunshine glinting off the way my hair moves. Then, whoever it is, scans to the left and right searching for possible threats.

Pssh, whoever they are, they don't seem to realize I'm the threat here, I think to myself, annoyed, I'm not seen as even a potential threat with the way they're barely watching me.

Then the eyes drift down to my hips moving back and forth as I walk, and the vision stays there locked on my butt, my hips moving back and forth like a pendulum as I walk.

Must be a man, great a male Fae. I roll my eyes as I feel my lips quirk up.

Then I'm hit like a ton of bricks. There is a male Fae stalking me. Why had I let down my guard so easily and found that funny? He is the enemy, and most likely here to kill me or follow me to Sanctuary and kill my people. I can't let this drag out. I need to end this now. I turn and loose an arrow to the left behind me where the Fae must be standing based on the visions I'm getting sent to me through his eyes.

22

ATTINA

As soon as the arrow leaves my hand, I am on the move, running as fast as my body will take me. I notice I can run faster than a normal human, but I still seriously doubt I can outrun a full-blooded Fae.

On the forefront of my mind the only thing pounding through my thoughts is Fae! A Fae found me! How is this possible? But in the back of my mind, I'm glad I sent Raven on her own path, but mad at myself at the same time because there would be no waiting for her to save me this time. I would rather die alone then let a Fae get their hands on Raven, bringing her back to Henrik. So, for the first time in my life I will have to get myself out of this danger.

Thank goodness Raven and I mapped out the town and surrounding areas beforehand. Father would be proud we followed his lessons. But then it hits me he can't be proud of us anymore because Father is gone. My eyes start to water as I run. I rub them and push those feelings down deep. Maybe someday I will have time to grieve for my father and Oak properly, but today is not that day.

I shake my head to clear my thoughts. I have to keep my mind sharp. I know my arrow hit the Fae because I heard him groan in pain, but he's chasing me, so he obviously moved out of the way too fast and my arrow missed its mark.

After checking out the area, I know there is an entrance to a canyon right outside of the North side of the city. I could run to Raven, but then I would lead this Fae right to her and who knows, he might try to take her from me.

I head to the canyon entrance at top speed, but I was right; he is faster than me. I take a quick glance back and take a deep intake of air, even with him slowed a little from being hit with an arrow he is gaining on me fast. Right as I reach the end of town, I hook a left running North. I will be out in the open for a few seconds, but I'll have to risk it.

From the quick glance I got of him, I don't think I saw a bow on the Fae so hopefully I've been lucky in that department. He hasn't tried to attack me back yet either, so all I can do is pray to the Gods he will simply continue to chase me. I can see the edge of the canyon opening about a hundred feet away. I think to myself, *just a little farther and hopefully I can lose him through the canyon trails.* On the way to the canyon there is a sloping tan sandy hill. When I'd seen it earlier, I had hoped I could get over it before the Fae could pass all of the buildings in the town, maybe I could even get over it before he saw where I had gone, but I wasn't so lucky. He knows exactly where I am.

Starting up the slope, I turn back and can't see him behind me, my legs are on fire but as I reach the top I glance behind me again and there he is at the bottom of the hill. No time to slow down now.

"Damn he's fast," I mutter to myself, pushing my legs to their limits.

As I run into the canyon, I glance back and he's barely

cresting the hill, a huge grin plastered on his face as he catches a last glimpse of me. I reach the path through the canyon cliffs and head into the red rock valley.

By now it's obvious I won't be able to outrun him. I'm going to have to fight him. I start searching for a decent place to make my stand. As I run, I notice a narrowing of the passage we're running down coming up. It's now or never.

Mid run I turn around and loose an arrow in the direction I think the Fae will be which he proceeds to slap out of his way midair like it's only an annoying fly not a deadly arrow. Throwing down my bow, I pull my sword out of its sheath, the beautifully engraved steel sparkling in the sunlight.

My opponent stops about ten feet from me and readjusts his tunic as if it being out of place was the biggest annoyance to him out of this whole situation. Not even bothering to acknowledge my existence, like I'm not even a threat.

Now, seeing him up close, I can see how gorgeous he is. He is the most beautiful man I have ever seen in my life. His shoulder length hair is dark, and reminds me of the color of Oak's tail. His eyes are a beautiful purple, which look like they can see into my soul, but are also so soft and childlike at the same time. His features are bulky and masculine. He wears what I can only describe as black fighting leathers. His massive muscles draw the leather tight. The only imperfection on him is a gleaming blood stain. I can barely discern on his right shoulder where my arrow hit it's mark. When he finally glances up, his mouth drops and he takes a step back like someone physically pushed him, then he just keeps standing there, in shock with his eyes locked on me.

"Why have you been following me?" I shout as I pull out my sword.

He doesn't answer for what feels like ages. He stands

there with his mouth hanging open, staring at me. Finally, he shakes his head like he's forcing himself out of a daydream and unsheathes his sword, but he stands there so long not moving I start to get annoyed by all this lack of movement. With all this standing around he must seriously not see me as a threat at all.

"Are we going to do this or not?" I snap at him lifting up my sword. My legs are shaking under me, but my face is stone, unflinching. I can't show him how scared I actually am. Letting him see my weakness would be the first step to letting him beat me.

The Fae smiles slyly like only he is privy to his own joke soaring over my stupid, slow human head.

"We certainly can, little kitten, but I'd rather know the name of my opponent, so I know what name to write on your tombstone." He smirks. He must be trying to goad me into charging him by insulting me so thoroughly. It won't work, I will not give in. I will not lose my head against him.

"Either fight or leave me alone, Fae," I say with venom on my lips.

"Fae?" he asks as he places his hand on his chest and takes a step back with a shocked hurt expression on his face like I'd slapped him.

"Well, that's what you are isn't it?"

"Yes, but you say it with such hatred, why would you hate us?" he asks in awe.

"Are you serious? Your people have murdered or enslaved almost the entire human race! You hunt my people down like cattle!" I yell incredulously.

"Your people?"

"Yes, my people!"

"Okay, but you're not human...at least not fully." He beams and winks at me.

"Yes, I am," I say, adjusting my grip on my sword.

"Lying is not a good look on you, little kitten," he says with his knowing smile spreading across his face. I want to knock that grin off his gorgeous face. Who is this Fae who acts like he knows me? What makes him think he has a right to question me like this?

"Who are you anyway?"

"Well, little kitten—"

"Stop calling me that!" I yell, interrupting him, which only serves to make his smile widen.

"Well, little kitten, my name is Allister," he says with an exaggerated bow putting his sword behind his back and bowing with a fist over his heart the flourish making him appear all the more like a gentleman. "And yes, I am Fae, I'm actually the king's number one slayer."

"Was," I growl with venom lacing my words.

"Was?" Allister says, confusion coating his words and a pout twisting his lips.

"You were the king's number one slayer." Then, before I realize what I'm doing, I rush right at him with my sword cutting through the air and a guttural scream on my lips.

Hearing the king mentioned is what did it. Even a passing mention of Henrik stirs a fiery hatred in me so much I lose control over my faculties and without thinking I attack. Father used to constantly tell me losing your head was a sure way to lose a fight. Now I will have to prove him wrong if I want to keep my head attached to my shoulders.

As my sword slices down hard on Allister I see a flash of metallic light and his sword appears there to meet mine. He sees my shock, and a shit-eating grin crawls across his face again. How is he moving this fast? I hit him with my arrow. The blood on his clothes proves it. He should be hurt but he moves like he's uninjured.

"Kitten has claws." His voice is smooth and seductive, his words slithering off his tongue and down my body like a snake marking its territory. My body begins to relax to the sound of his voice. I physically shake off that false sense of security.

"You're damn straight kitten has claws," I spout off seething with anger from the way my body reacts to his voice.

He meets my each and every move with grace and perfection, but doesn't move in for the attack, like he's testing my skill as a swords woman more than trying to actually beat me.

"You move faster than a human should be able to. I wonder why, since you say you're human," Allister says with that smirk still plastered on his face. We parry again, faster and faster. He's obviously trying to prove a point by making me move faster than a human could dream to move to keep up with his strikes.

"I don't know what you're saying, I'm just a human," I lie and even I hear it for the lie it is.

At this, he throws himself at me, flipping through the air. I take a step back and he's flying over my head, his head mere inches from mine.

As he is perpendicular to me he brings down his sword, giving me half a second to respond. I throw up my sword and move to the left, moving so his sword glances off mine. The blade narrowly misses me as it deflects off the edge of my sword away from my body. Then he lands directly behind me where I'd been standing seconds ago. He's facing away from me, but as he pivots to face me, another smug smile slowly crosses his face.

"I knew it! You're definitely Fae. There's no way you're all human after seeing that maneuver of yours. No humans can move as fast as you just did, my attack would've been a killing strike to any human, and low and behold, kitten, you're still alive. So, that begs the question why lie?"

I glare at Allister, which of course only serves to egg him on.

"So, what do you have to hide, why would you deny being Fae? More importantly, why in the world would you despise your own people so much?" The breath is knocked out of me with his words. I fight the urge to walk over to him and spill all of my secrets to him. What the hell is happening?

I see a split in the rock wall behind me and I stumble backwards a few steps into it. I need a place to hide from Allister just for a second. I need to gather my thoughts. My body and head are at war. My body calls to him, but my brain tells me he is Fae and can't be trusted. My heart wants to tell him everything. Who my mother was, what my plan is, everything, but my head knows spilling everything would be like wrapping a noose around my own throat.

The cut in the canyon is deep so I can crawl in and get far enough away from Allister to where he can't reach me with his sword. I move backwards slowly, not truly paying attention to where my feet are traveling, my mind unbalanced with uncertainty, as I take my next step, I feel claws wrap around my ankle right above my boot.

The nails dig deep into my flesh, I cry out and as I glance down to see what has a hold of me. Teeth break through my skin. Glancing down, I see blood dripping down my leg. The rotten lips pulled back to show the black, rotting gums, and attached to those gums, are brown, cracked, jagged fangs. Those incisors are now buried in my leg. The pain hits me and I scream like a rabbit in the jaws of a wolf. Then I take my sword and bury it in the disgusting thing's head, while letting out a war cry for the life, which is now going to be taken from me.

Putting my back against the hard red rock wall, I slide down into a sitting position. The rock ripping down my back grounds me. I somehow have the presence of mind to chuck my mother's sword down deeper into the dark crevice I've found myself in. As I watch it soar through the air, tears fill my eyes. I feel like my heart is being ripped out of my chest. Like everything I've recently learned about my mother is being cleaved out of me. One of the only things I've ever had of my mother's is now lost forever. I remind myself it's better lost than used to kill humans by a Fae.

I turn to the right as I'm sliding, and see the monster. The Solis who has taken my life, my body just doesn't know it yet. At one point, the Solis was a woman, but the lower half of her body is smashed like she'd fallen from the top of the canyon and broke all the bones in the lower half of her body from the plummet. Before becoming a Solis, she had flaxen brown hair and stunning green eyes, those eyes now vacant in her death. I would've bet my life before the flesh had started falling off her body she had been a stunning woman.

As soon as my butt touches the ground, a breeze braces me from my left. I know that it's Allister beside me before I even turn my head. My body instantly relaxes from his close proximity, which flusters and frustrates me. I know he wants to kill me, but at this point it would be a mercy, at least he could give me a quick end. Hopefully, he will give me the relief of sticking his sword through my brain so I won't have to turn into a Solis myself.

"Well little kitten, you seem to have gotten yourself into a bind. Haven't you ever heard curiosity killed the cat?"

Before I realize it, words are pouring out of my mouth. "Finish the quote. Satisfaction brought it back." I don't know why, but I can't stop myself from being a smartass to him, even now.

"Well, aren't you a smart cookie."

"Unlike you," I snap. I take a deep intake of air, calming my temper. I need to cool it. I need his help. "Please. I beg you, warrior to warrior, please kill me so I won't turn into one of those things," I say, pointing to the dead Solis. Allister cocks his head, and his brows draw together in confusion.

"Now, why would I want to do such a thing?"

"It's the decent thing to do, and my dying wish," I seethe.

"But then I wouldn't be able to see what happens to you, little kitten, when you get bit by something made of Fae," Allister bubbles out as he slides down next to me and pulls my head into his lap. I don't fight it, I let him pull me to him, needing the comfort of another person next to me. His fighting leathers are curiously soft and his warmth is surprisingly comforting.

I don't understand him. He was trying to kill me a second ago and now he wants to hold me then watch as I change into a Solis? What is he getting out of this? Is he so sick and demented he truly only wants to torture me? It doesn't matter now though, either way I'm about to die.

"Fine then just leave me to die in peace, you nasty Fae bastard!" I snap but don't move out of his warm embrace needing to not be alone right now.

Allister laughs. Then he says, "Well, aren't you a dramatic kitten."

"Stop fucking calling me kitten!" I scream, then the pain

hits me like a ton of bricks, the excruciating, mind numbing pain. It feels like my Awakening is starting all over again.

I let out a wail like an animal being tortured and move out of Allister's lap needing the hard earth to stabilize me. I lay down on the auburn dirt ground. The cool earth on my face is grounding me. The pain is zapping away my energy, I have no more will to argue, and then through the haze of pain, I hear Allister.

"Well, if you don't want me to call you kitten anymore what's your name?" I can hear something akin to worry dripping from his voice. Why in the world is this bastard Fae worried? The pain must be messing with my head. I am nothing but a mouse to him, a mouse to play with before killing.

"Why do you care what my name is? I'm dying, it won't matter anymore."

"Actually, your name matters quite a great deal to me," he says in a matter-of-fact way.

I turn my head towards him, using my last bit of energy to send him one last gleaming glare. At this Allister throws his head back and laughs a deep, velvety, booming laugh. He almost appears like a normal human when he's relaxed like this. If it wasn't for his gorgeous, glittering purple eyes and those pointy ears of his I might have been fooled.

"Stop thinking about my eyes and tell me your name, beautiful kitten," Allister purrs out.

I have no more fight left in me anymore, so I whisper, "Attina."

Then all I see is darkness. I hear Allister repeat my name, and his hand lovingly caresses my face. Hearing my name on his lips is like pure bliss. It sounds sensual and right. Like he's the only person in the world who should be saying my name.

With my last moments of consciousness, I can only think how strangely my life has turned out. I'd always known dying was a big possibility; hell, this was a suicide mission. But I never once thought I would have a Fae sitting sympathetically by my side sounding worried for me as I fade into darkness. Allister's steady breathing ushering me into the afterlife.

23

ATTINA

"Attina!"

"Attina!"

"Attina, wake up! Oh god, please no!"

I slowly blink my eyes open. My vision is so blurred at first all I can discern is the general shape of a man. His muscular biceps come into clarity first. I can feel I'm in someone's arms, but the warmth I felt when I was in Allister's arms is gone.

"Allister?" I whisper.

Then I'm being squished against the canyon wall, my ribs feeling like they are about to explode from all the pressure being put on them.

"You're alive!"

"Attina it's me, James."

"Big ears?" I croak out, confused. The haze in my vision begins to clear and I see his rounded jaw, his brown eyes and those same big ears I'd grown up making fun of. I raise my hand up to touch his ears and feel him chuckle.

"Seriously, Attina? After what you've been through you want to pick on my ears right now? Well, you're definitely the same girl I grew up with. I thought you were dead Attina, I saw you lying unconscious next to this Solis and I knew you were done for." Tears fill his eyes as he speaks. "But look at you! You're fine! I don't know how you are okay but thank the God's you're alive."

"James what's going on? How did you find me?"

"I was on a supply run with my team when we spotted a Fae. There were ten of us against one Fae. My whole team and I are being combat trained, so as a team we decided to chase after it."

"Allister," I whisper to myself thinking of that beautiful bastard. So, he led James and his team to me. He helped me. Why would he do something so risky? I thought he wanted me dead. Why not just kill me? James keeps rambling on with his story, completely ignoring the fact that I've said another man's name again.

"We had him on the run. I knew we had the numbers on him, and we chased him into this canyon. Then he went down the alley we're in now and I figured he'd made the biggest mistake of his life when I realized he ran into a dead end.

I yelled to my team, "We have him dead to rights! When I turned down the alley he'd disappeared, but you were the only thing in this alley, just laying on the ground unconscious next to this dead Solis. I thought you were dead, then all of a sudden, I see your chest barely moving and I realized you were breathing! I checked you over for a bite and I saw you'd been bitten in the leg so I panicked and started screaming. I thought I was losing you all over again. I picked you up in my arms and yelled for you. You must've heard me somewhere, fought off the change and you came back to me!" At this point, James is crying, big creeks of tears rolling down his face like he'd seen a miracle.

I lay there on the ground in his arms and all I can do is laugh. I cackle so loudly that James gives a start like I physically slapped him. James' face turns from one of pure happiness to one of shock and worry and he starts shaking me and screaming, "Attina! Attina, are you okay? Are you changing? What's going on?"

I scream back, "No, you idiot!"

Instantly his face changes to one of fury, and he glares at me with rage flashing through his eyes. I can almost see the red blaze in his brown eyes, but after everything I've been through these past weeks, his anger doesn't deter me one bit. If anything, it fuels my fire.

"You seriously think I fought off turning into a Solis to get back to you? This isn't some fairytale," I snap, annoyed at his ridiculous assumption.

James stares at me incredulously. "Then what happened? You obviously got bit and you haven't turned," he says, pointing at my ankle.

I pull down my pant leg, covering the bite as I take in a deep steadying breath. I knew going into this adventure at some point I would have to tell him the truth but how will he take this? He hates Fae at least as much as I did. I've known him my whole life, and he deserves the truth, but will this make him hate me? I swallow the lump in my throat before diving headfirst into the truth.

"James you know my mother died a few months after giving birth to me, or at least that's what I was told."

"Yes... What are you saying? Is your mother alive?"

"Well, she was until about a week ago." I stop for a second glancing down at the red dry dirt next to me. Then I peek back up to James and say the words, which flipped my world upside down these past few weeks.

"She was Fae, James. I'm part Fae"

James drops me out of his lap, and I tumble hard onto the ground. He jumps up and away from me like I'm contagious; like if he touches me for too long, he might become Fae too. I sit up, stare at him, and plead.

"Please just hear me out James—" I say while putting my hands out like I'm trying to calm a wild animal.

I tell him the whole story exactly as I'd heard it from my Father. I tell him everything that's happened to me since we last saw each other. Halfway through the story, he sits down against the opposite wall facing me, keeping his distance, making sure our bodies don't touch. He doesn't say one word until I am finished with my story. His eyes are as big as dinner plates while I'm talking, but as soon as the story is through, James takes a long breath and glances at me with his soft eyes.

He crawls over to where I'm sitting and wraps his arms around me. "Well, I already promised myself to you so I guess I'll figure out a way to get past this." Then he puts his arm around my waist and helps lift me up off of the ground, but as soon as I'm up on my own two feet everything goes dark again.

24

———

ATTINA

I'm running away; from what, I have no idea. I see a huge hill in front of me and all I can think is I have to run up this hill, I have to get away.

Up, up, up. The hill turns into an unending mountain. My legs ache and my calves groan against the pressure pushed on them. I just need to make it to the other side of this gargantuan mountain. I can do it. Only a little further—

I wake with a start, my whole body aches and sweat pours off of me. I feel like my insides are too big to fit inside my chest. It's so dark wherever I am. I'm lying on what I assume is a bed with a pillow under my head and blankets over me. To my shock and embarrassment, I realize I'm only in my underwear. Someone must have put me to bed and undressed me while I was unconscious.

I hear shuffling outside of the room I'm in, and what I assume is a door to my left shakes. I jump out of bed groping for anything I can use to defend myself. It's too dark in here to see much except the outlines of objects.

Not finding anything, I steel myself for hand-to-hand

combat. I think to myself, *keep calm Attina, you can do this, you are a warrior. Father trained you for this.*

The door creaks open and I throw my hands up, ready for whatever or whoever is about to walk through that door.

First thing I see is the light illuminating from a candle that someone's hand is holding. I sneak over to the door so when it opens completely, I can be positioned behind it, and behind my attacker. A figure walks through the doorway. I see rounded ears and thick muscle corded arms, so it must be a male human.

I take in a deep, steadying breath of air and throw my punch. My punch lands on the base of the man's skull. The mystery man falls down to his knees, I can hear the crack of his knees landing against the hard rock floor as the man grabs at his head.

Before he can get up, I have my legs wrapped around his middle and my arm is snatched around his throat in a choke hold Father showed me during one of our training sessions. Then I hear it. A choking sound.

"Attina! It's me, Attina! Let me go!"

It takes a second for those words to sink in. Then the voice finally registers in my mind. With my arms still wrapped around his neck I ask, "James?" The man nods his head a fraction and pats my arm in a defeated gesture. I release him, unhooking my legs from him and I back away.

James kneels on the ground for a minute rubbing at his throat, regaining the breath I stole out of his lungs. The candle James brought into the room is on the ground now, but by some miracle it's still lit. The metal candlestick holder also didn't break after falling to the rock-hard ground. So, I step over to the candle and pick it up, leaving James on the ground while he gathers his wits.

I walk around the room with the candle in my hand,

checking out my surroundings. The room appears to be cut out of some form of red rock. It appears to be the same rock the canyon Allister and I fought in was made of. There is a wash basin on the wall, across from the door. The bed is on a rock slab cut into the wall. A wardrobe is standing across the room from the bed with my sword leaning up against it. I walk around the small room, but it is only the bare essentials, and windowless, no wonder it was so dark without the candlelight.

By the time I'm done checking out my meager surroundings, James has collected himself and is standing by the now closed door, staring at me. I glance down, only now remembering I'm only in my underwear.

Now James's hungry, predatory stare reminds me how close to naked I actually am. I throw my hands up, almost burning myself with the candle as I try to cover my body in embarrassment. I don't want him leering at me like that, it makes me feel like a piece of meat he wants to consume.

James prowls over to me. "Do you remember what happened, Attina?" James says in an oily, wrong voice I've never heard leave his lips before.

I back away from James's approach until my thighs hit the edge of the bed. I stand there with my arms wrapped meekly around my body with what I know is a muddled expression on my face, thinking. *How did I get here? What's the last thing I remember?* I remember fighting that Fae, he was taunting me, Allister. He knew I wasn't technically human. Then I got bit.

I take a deep breath and my glance drifts down to my leg where the Solis bit me. Even in the candlelight I can tell the bite is still extremely red and angry James smirks at me with a menacing grin framing his face. His eyes travel excruciatingly slowly from the bite on my ankle up my body and his gaze sticks to my breasts. I wrap my arms around myself tighter. I hate the way he's ogling at me. He's staring at me like I'm his coveted possession.

James cuts in. "You remember now?".

"Yes James, I remember. Where are we? Where is my horse and why are you looking at me like that?"

"You made it to Sanctuary, and I don't know where *your* horse is, but we have your father's horse here in the stables at the compound. She found us shortly after you passed out in my arms."

"Sanctuary, so we're underground." I instantly feel a wave of claustrophobia at the realization. I take in a deep breath, calming myself and continue, "The compound? What's that?"

His mouth turns up into a snarl and he prowls over to me slowly, his hands fisted the entire time. "Who's Allister?" he asks through clenched teeth.

Hearing Allister's name spit out of his mouth with such venom shocks me.

"How do you know that name?" I say with more alarm and confusion than I want.

"That's the name you called for when you first woke up after I found you. You called to him like he would save you. You haven't ever called for me like that before."

I can hear the anger in his voice and now with him standing right in front of me I can see the anger coating his features. What scares me the most is the unending hatred I can see written in his eyes. The anger making his whole body shake.

"Allister is just someone I met while I was on the road to you." James stares at me questioningly. I lift my hands and blurt out with more exaggerated force, "He's no one. I promise. Only the last person I had contact with before being bit."

James reaches his hands out to caress my arms. I try not to flinch from his touch as his hands strokes me. His caress is soft, dragging down my arms until he gets to my wrists, then he grabs and squeezes my wrists with so much force and anger it feels like he might crush them.

He's so much stronger than I am even with my Fae blood coursing through me, his rage must be making him inhumanly strong. I try to rip my wrists away but it only serves to make him hang on tighter.

I yell, "James let me go of me! You're hurting me."

His eyes darken as he says in a deep composed voice, "No Attina, you are mine." He growls.

"James you're scaring me, what's going on?" I cry out.

James stares at me with a blank, dark expression on his face. His smile turns into a malicious grin, as he holds onto me tighter.

His voice takes on a deathly cold tone "Attina, you are mine whether you realize it or not. You are *mine*."

My mind is running a mile a minute. There are so many questions flipping through my thoughts. Why is he acting like this? Has something happened? Did he change, or was he always like this and I just didn't see it?

I coo with the most soothing voice I can muster. "Okay James, I'm yours. I've always been yours."

At hearing this his shoulders sag like a weight has been lifted and he pulls me into his arms. James whispers in my ear, "You are mine, Attina."

As he leans his head against my shoulder, I feel my own lower, and the tension I hadn't noticed before, leaves me.

"Yes James, I'm yours," I reiterate.

James leans over and presses his lips hard to mine. It

feels like he's trying to claim me, and I let him, for now. Whatever I just saw spill out of him scares me. It isn't the James I know. It is something inhuman.

His kiss deepens as he pushes me back toward the bed as I feel his need for me growing. I get it, he's claiming me, but this is not happening right now.

I sit down on the bed, breaking our kiss and glance up to him.

"I'm really not in the mood tonight."

His eye's flash and the craziness from a second ago is slowly coming back before my very own eyes but I push on.

"I've had a rough couple of weeks. Can I just rest?" Almost as an afterthought I add, "You can stay and we can cuddle." I try to force some hopefulness into my voice.

James' eyes soften. He cups my head gently between his hands.

"Yes of course we can cuddle. You must be exhausted after what you've been through. We can always get reacquainted when you're well and rested up." His eyes fill with something close to anticipation before softening again.

He pulls back the sheets and lets me crawl in. Then he shucks off his clothes down to his underwear and follows me into bed.

"Go ahead and rest now, you're safe," he whispers in my ear.

I'm not sure I believe him, but I am utterly exhausted. I'm completely on edge after what just happened. No matter how much James just scared me, my body knows his and it relaxes almost as soon as James settles in next to me and wraps his arm around my midsection. My eyelids quickly grow heavy, and I fall into a fretful night's sleep.

25

JAMES

As soon as Attina relaxes next to me I feel myself unwind. She's been through so much, I shouldn't be acting like this, but I can't seem to help myself, I've been worried about her since the townspeople, and I left Daruk.

When Nathan told me before we left town that Silas took Attina on one last father and daughter camp out, I was livid. I couldn't believe Silas took Attina away from me without asking. Nathan was able to calm me down, however. He said Silas and Attina would be right behind us and reassured me Silas could take care of them, but obviously that wasn't true.

Before I stumbled upon Attina on my team's mission, I'd been begging my commander to send a search party to find her, but he consistently shut down the idea. He'd say one rogue person who wasn't even one of Sanctuary's citizens didn't warrant a whole search party. I had even talked to him about it the day I found her.

Then when I found her, I went through every emotion you can think of in those few seconds it took me to realize she was okay. I walked down that small rock corridor and when I laid eyes on her lifeless body, I felt so broken and devastated, like the last bit of me had died away.

My family was taken away from me as a child and there was nothing I could do about it. Then I saw Attina lying there on the ground and I thought I'd lost the last piece of my family forever. I lost my mind for a moment, and started screaming her name over and over.

Right as I was vowing to burn down the world for taking everything I love from me, her chest started slightly rising and falling. When I saw her breathing, I felt the happiest feeling I've ever felt in my life; but I was also more scared than I've ever been. She has obviously been bitten by the Solis that was next to her. She was coming back to me but was she coming back as Attina or as a Solis creature?

Her eyes focused on me and I knew it was Attina, not a Solis in my arms. As soon as I realized she was still herself, I was so happy I cried out of pure bliss, until she called out for another man.

Who the hell is this Allister?

She said she called his name out because he was the last person she saw before she was bitten but I don't believe it.

I know Attina better than she knows herself, and she wouldn't ever call out some random man's name. The jealous monster, who lives inside me has been scratching at the back of my mind since the moment another man's name slipped from her lips.

When I saw her tonight the first thing she did was attack me, clad in only her underwear no less. She should have been vulnerable the way I left her in just her underwear, but she attacked me. When I realized she again didn't need me, the jealous monster just broke out of its cage. There was no turning back after that, but I'm not sorry for it.

She is *mine* and she obviously needs to be reminded of the fact.

My parents left me, but she doesn't ever get to leave me. Only the death of her or me will allow either of us to leave. I will die before I let anyone, including her, take my family from me ever again.

As she sleeps, she shakes restlessly. I brush some rogue hairs behind her ear so I can look at her face. I smile as I see how beautiful she is. She's mine, and finally here in my arms. I can't believe it.

I know it's her dream to travel the world and find new adventures, but she's so young, she doesn't actually know what she wants. We will get married and before she knows it we'll have a few kids and those dreams of adventures in far off places will be gone forever. She'll be happy taking care of her family; I know it. Besides she's kidding herself if she thinks I'm ever going to let her leave. If she thinks I'm ever letting her go back out in such a dangerous world, she has another thing coming.

It's time for us to settle down, get serious, and become a real family.

EPILOGUE

Allister

After what's seemed like months, I'm back in this dark chamber. I walk back into the throne room, and all of Henrik's soldiers' golden heads turn toward me.

Under my arm, I carry Attina's fascinating bow and quiver set. I'd wanted to grab her sword with the Fae runes on it; she was wielding so inexpertly. But once she got bit by the Solis and killed it, she somehow had the presence of mind to fling her sword away before I got to her. I searched, but I couldn't find where it clattered off to before those humans got close enough for me to lead them to her.

The thought of her throwing it somewhere I couldn't find it makes me smile. She's absolutely full of fire.

This bow was obviously made by Fae hands, and after Attina passed out, I was able to smear some of her blood on it. Now, it smells like her. I'm guessing Henrik knows the half Fae's scent, and hopefully it will be enough to convince

Henrik I killed her. It's not much but I'm hoping he'll want her dead so badly he'll just believe me.

Sounds like a lot of hoping in my plan but it's all I've got.

I stop at the foot of the dais and place my fisted hand over my chest as I bow to Henrik, then nod over to my blank-faced mother.

"Is it done?" Henrik's booming voice fills the room.

"Yes, sire. I've brought back her bow. I gutted her and her blood spilled all over it." I give him a wicked grin, absolutely looking the part of the bloodthirsty, evil, obedient Fae he expects me to be.

Henrik nods his head as he glares down to the bow in my hand, a sinister grin spreading across his face. He lifts his hand in a dismissing gesture. "Good. You're excused."

I bow again, but keep my feet planted.

"You dare defy me?" Anger rides his booming voice and fire flares in his eyes.

I kneel down on one knee. "Never, but I have one more thing I wish to speak to you about."

"Then spit it out," his tone bored.

"I may have found a human stronghold." Henrik sits up. I guess I got his attention now.

"You what?" Surprise coating his voice.

"Yes, sire. A human man happened to stumble along after I killed the half-breed. He must've known her because he cried, and then took the body with him. I followed him out of curiosity.

He went back to a huge canyon carved out of the earth. I followed him to a dead end where he disappeared into thin air. There must be a hidden door there. If the whispers about a human stronghold are true, that could be where it's located."

Henrik strokes his chin and thinks on what I said for a

second before he opens his mouth. "While I find it hard to believe a sizable group of humans could've survived unnoticed this long, I don't like the fact that a human disappeared with the half breed's body. There is a small chance they could be a threat." He places his head on his fist on the armrest of his throne.

"I want you to investigate and see what you can find. I want reconnaissance Allister, only reconnaissance. Once you've gathered enough information, report back directly to me."

"Yes, sire." I dip my head and rise.

"Take your time. See if you can find out the intricacies of that place, whatever it is. I have faith in you. You will help me crush those humans once and for all."

I bow to him. "Yes, sire. Nothing would make me happier. I will not fail you." I stand to my full height and with a newfound confidence, I turn and walk out of the room. I'm surprised at how our conversation played out.

"You better not." I hear him roar from behind me.

As I leave the throne room, I let out a huge exhale. Somehow that went exactly the way I'd planned, the Gods must be with me tonight. Now I have time to figure out my next move. I glance down at the bow and smile.

But first, I have to return this to its owner.

The End

OTHER BOOKS BY CAITLIN DENMAN

She Rises coming Winter 2021

ABOUT THE AUTHOR

Caitlin lives and grew up in Southern California with her family and her three horses, three dogs, and a cat. She graduated from Cal Poly Pomona with a bachelor's in agribusiness.

Besides writing, she loves training and competing on horses. She has competed in barrel racing, breakaway roping, team roping, and mounted shooting. She has owned and ridden horses since she was twelve-years-old.

Caitlin would love to connect with each and every person who loves her books. You can find her on Facebook or Instagram at the links below
or email her at:
caitilindenmanbooks@gmail.com

ACKNOWLEDGMENTS

Thank you again to my parents. This book never would have seen the light of day without you guys. Thank you for being there to bounce ideas off of, supporting me through my ups and downs, and for being some of my first beta readers.

I want to thank my baby Rilynn just for being born. You made me want to write this story of a girl overcoming hardships and coming out stronger in the end. I hope when times get tough you read this and remember how strong, smart, and beautiful you are little one.

Next, I want to thank Paul Smith for being for being my rock through all the ups and downs that came with writing this. You were always a shoulder to cry on.

I also want to thank my editor Amy Briggs. Without her taking me step by step through the publication process, I fully believe this book would have stayed on my computer for the rest of my life.

Finally I want to thank all of my friends and family who were there with me on this journey letting me bounce ideas off of you, reading bits and pieces, and pushing me to finish this huge project.

Thank you to every single person who helped bring this
book to life!

www.ingramcontent.com/pod-product-compliance
Lightning Source LLC
Chambersburg PA
CBHW021148110726
47900CB00002B/475